GM & GS PRIVATE INVESTIGATION SERVICE

BOOK III

D. H. CROSBY

authorHOUSE®

AuthorHouse™
1663 Liberty Drive
Bloomington, IN 47403
www.authorhouse.com
Phone: 1 (800) 839-8640

Published by AuthorHouse 03/07/2017

ISBN: 978-1-5246-7527-1 (sc)
ISBN: 978-1-5246-7526-4 (e)

PART NINE

CHAPTER ONE

Madeline was devastated. She had sent Adriana into a spiral all because of what she had asked. I can't believe she didn't know, but how could she.

Marcus Buchanan was Adriana's father. He had said at the dinner the other night at the closing of his buying GM & GS OIL REFINERIES, that she had not spoken to him in three years.

This was about Unitus. She hated it for him. She could see he really loved Adriana. Her reaction was a woman betrayed. She must have thought he had something to do with the business deal.

This girl was not thinking straight. Unitus had not been to visit them ever. He was Bruce's friend, and she had not spoken to her son in five years until recently.

It was so sad. Jana was crying and Bruce could not get Unitus to follow Adriana. He had said, "She will not believe anything I would say."

Trevor put his arm around Madeline to comfort her.

"This has been a homecoming to remember. Just know you did nothing wrong, my dear. Adriana will realize it sooner or later. For Unitus's sake I hope it will be sooner."

"I want to see the babies. That will cheer me up," Madeline said and Trevor agreed.

He got their coats and they drove up the bend to Guy's house first. She wanted to see her Kyleigh. She was met by Mrs. Middleton, Kyleigh's mother.

"Come on in. So good to see you," she said.

Madeline said, "I have being dying to see that baby. I'm glad you were here to help her."

Mrs. Middleton said, "This is the first time for me, too. We couldn't get out in the snow to go to the hospital. He is so precious."

They walked up the stairs to the nursery leaving the husbands behind to chat.

There Kyleigh sat in her rocker-glider breastfeeding the baby. Madison Kyle Smith was enjoying his meal. He had his eyes closed and was suckling with both little hands trying to cup his mama's tiny breast.

Madeline kissed Kyleigh on top of her head saying, "He is a beautiful baby, but I knew he would be, if he took after his mother." Smiling at Kyleigh as if no time had past since their last visit.

"Well your grandson is pretty handsome, too. He has been so upset that he was not here for me. I know he came as soon as he could," Kyleigh just could not get pass it.

This was the second time, he was not there for her. The first time was the kidnapping which she had began having flash-backs about recently. The doctor said him not being with her during the birth ... had triggered their return.

"Kyleigh ... he loves you! If the airport had not been closed, he would have flown home sooner."

Mrs. Middleton said, "He shouldn't have gone in the first place!"

"OMG mother! Stop right now, please!" Kyleigh begged putting the baby on her shoulder to burp him.

"Guy had to go to sign the papers, so his company could be sold. He had to go! It was for Kyleigh and the baby that he went Mrs. M.?" Madeline was getting riled.

After what had happened earlier, she was not in the mood to listen to this woman. A woman who had never worked a day in her life, and had completely ignored her own daughter's upbringing. She was so glad she had been there for Kyleigh. Madeline hugged Kyleigh.

Kyleigh pressed the intercom button, "Guy can you ask daddy to take MOTHER home. Thank you, Honey!"

"So I am to be escorted out when she comes in, I have no problem leaving!" she stomped out as her husband reached the top of the stairs.

"What have you done now?" he said.

"Take me home," she was blowing her nose into one of her finely embroidered handkerchiefs that she had handmade. She always had time for everything in the past except for Kyleigh.

Madeline had been the one that took care of Kyleigh when she was young. Whenever Kyleigh had needed a mother, she would run to GM's house. This, Mrs. Middletton knew, and resented.

"Can I hold him?" Madeline asked. He was smiling and wiggling. Trevor came up behind her and was goo- gooing and he kissed Kyleigh on the forehead.

Trevor said, "He's got gas. That is a mighty big smile young man," playing with the baby's toes.

Guy said, "Can I get you ladies anything? If not I will see them out to the garage," Kyleigh waved for him to go.

He took them down the back elevator in silence. He knew his father-in-law was dealing with his wife's bad behavior.

"Come back anytime. I will be with her from now on," Guy was trying to reassure Mrs. Middleton.

"Good!" she got in the car and they drove off.

He went back up to see the family enjoying his little one.

Madeline and Trevor stayed thirty minutes and caught up on the details and explained, they had to go to Roscoe's next. Hugs and kisses followed. A kiss blown by Madeline that Guy caught and slapped on the back of his neck. It had always been their special sign of love through the years.

When they got to Roscoe's he came running to them I am so glad to see you, hugging each. "Follow me … we are stuck on the second floor. Beatrice wants an elevator … now HA HA!"

Roscoe kissed his wife and the boys were finally quiet.

He looked at them grinning, "Aren't they angels?"

"They are very handsome. Just like my Roscoe," Madeline patting Roscoe on the cheek.

Beatrice was squirming in bed, like did you forget me over here. Roscoe kissed her red hair and looked into her pale green eyes, "Yes, you are my special angel sent from heaven above!" He must remember to include her in any comment because those hormones were still raging.

Trevor said, "I think they have Beatrice's hair color and smile," he knew how to say the right thing. Beatrice was beaming at her twins and in-laws.

Beatrice was squeezing Roscoe's hand tightly.

"I know Roscoe wants to ask you both for some help! So now is the time because the twins are asleep. In about three hours Roscoe will have his hands full," she smiled up at him.

"Isn't she great? She reads minds so watch out!"

"What can we do for you Roscoe?" Trevor asked.

He told them about Tate, the boy he had met at the library. How he was abandoned by his family and that his aunt had took him in. Madeline nodded. She understood what Roscoe was saying. It really was … just like you … did for me.

He paused to hug Madeline that had got all misty eyed. Trevor felt like it was their moment to revisit and bond, so he walked to a picture and began looking at it.

He continued that Tate is new in town and this girl attached herself to him. As a friend, she asked him to help protect her.

"GM … Trevor … this girl was gang raped by the football team. I have placed her in a battered shelter, but here's the hard part, I am wanting to get a conviction." He paced.

"The Social Worker and my buddy on the police force are helping, but I know if we don't play this right … They will kill the boy for interfering and the girl is already a target. I know you 'all have just got home. I have got my hands full here and work, but I can't stand by and let these punks get away with this. They will continue to harm innocent people. They have to be STOPPED."

Trevor said, "You know we are in, son … we will talk tomorrow. GM looks so tired. It's been a long day since we left Dallas," looking at Madeline.

"Love to all. I'll say goodnight!" She kissed Roscoe and blew a kiss at Beatrice.

Then they were home, showered and fell into bed.

"Well I guess GM & GS Private Investigation Service is still needed in this town. We could reopen?" Madeline said.

"Goodnight dear!" Trevor said and soon he began to snore.

Madeline's wheels were turning when sleep finally came.

When the morning rose across the mountains and the coffee was brewing, Madeline was writing a storyboard on a pad.

Trevor asked, "What you got there?" peering over her bare shoulder. He kissed it and pulled her robe up to cover it.

"You'll caught your death of cold!" Trevor replied looking into her eyes.

"Since when have you wanted to warm me up this way? Usually you are taking my clothes off?" Madeline surmised.

"Since we have company standing behind you!" He said.

She spewed her coffee laughing and was dabbing it off her bathrobe with a kitchen towel.

Then Bruce and Jana appeared and sat down with them at the breakfast nook.

"Don't mind us mother. I may gnaw on Jana any minute," and he grabbed a cup of java and smiled at her. She threw the towel at Trevor who was chuckling.

"I'm going to check on the dogs and see how much damage that bear did," he was halfway out the door.

"Good try, mister! Come back here and face the music! Help little old me … fix breakfast and I may forget about fixing you!"

Madeline was wielding a kitchen knife as if she may neuter him any minute.

"Yes, madam. You want scrambled or poached eggs?" Trevor knew what her answer would be.

"Scramble them ... but good," and she winked at him. Jana said, "Grab your coffee. Let's go! We will be late!"

Bruce looked stunned, "OH yeah!" Right!"

She told Madeline they had promised Beatrice that they would help her with the twins this morning. Then they would help Kyleigh which she probably won't need help. Since she has Guy home all day, every day.

Jana admitted, "We just have to see Madison!"

Madeline said and waved them out, "GO! GO! Do what you have to do."

"Bruce wants to check on Unitus. My heart hurts for him. So I may be at Beatrice's until he gets back. If you need me, just text. Love you! KISS! KISS!" and they were gone.

Unitus could not stay there and he definitely could not go back to White Rock Lake in Dallas. So he was staying at Grandma's old home in Hendersonville. Madeline insisted. Bruce had Guy settle him in.

Unitus had only this one week till his assignment would begin. He had to get his head on straight.

Bruce told him, "Man ... you need to skip this one! Call in sick ... Tell them anything! Just don't go ... I need you to wait for me."

Unitus replied, "Yeah right. You can't go anywhere for six months ... and you know it! I am about crazy over Adriana, but she will have settled down by the time your court case comes up and I will see her then. I will be here," pointing to the floor. "Till end of this week resting and thinking, so if you want to come by and have a beer or go shoot some pool, let me know! Otherwise leave me be. I'll be fine."

"Okay, if you want to talk you know my number!" chest bumping him and a big brotherly hug. Then he was gone.

Unitus was settling in when Roscoe came by, "Just wanted to see… if you needed anything?"

Unitus said, "Yeah I do. Where is the nearest gym?"

"No problem follow me!" and he jumped in the Silverado.

"I can't keep asking people to drive me around. I first need to go by and rent me something to drive for the remainder of the week. Then to the gym and another important thing where are the restaurants?"

He called Beatrice and told her.

"Take your time, darling. Bruce and Jana are here . I'll tell them and they will stay. Kiss Unitus for us!"

He ate with Unitus and let him talk. He was a listener and it was an outpouring. Roscoe had never hear a man so in love with a woman. "Sounds like me and Beatrice. She came to Guy's wedding and sweep me off my feet the first day, too!"

They fist bumped and continued eating.

"Unitus said, "You know when it is the one!"

"Dang! If that ain't so… we have not been apart since. You and Adriana will reunite and I want you to bring her back. This is a good little town. We'd love to be your neighbor," Roscoe suggested.

"Thank you Roscoe, but she would never come back here. Nor would I want her to … I still see her face …she hates me! She didn't want to come, but I made her. I just wanted her to meet my family. Bruce and Jana are all I got." Unitus sipped his beer and finished his burger.

"Not any more! You have me and Beatrice, Guy and Kyleigh, Trevor and Madeline. Sounds to me like you got a BIG family here!" Roscoe meant every word and said it.

"I mean every word Unitus," Roscoe shook his hand and went on home.

Unitus had a jeep rented and the directions to the only gym in town. Where he went and paid for a week, got a locker and stashed his gear. He was too full and too tired, he decided to go back and get some sleep ... some much needed sleep.

CHAPTER TWO

"We have to talk!" Adriana told her father. She had stomped into his office without warning. The receptionist had tried to stop her once in the past. She knew better than getting in her way this time, there was fire in this girl's eyes. Marcus was sitting behind his massive desk with his feet propped up and smoking one of his fine Cuban cigars. In came a tornado, none could compare to this one. His daughter Adriana was known for her dramatics in the family and in the courtroom.

"Now what have I done?" her father asked. It was always something, he had done to displease her. She took after him. She would not spare anyone's feelings, if she thought she was right. That's my girl. Of all his children, she was his favorite ... probably because she stood up to him when the others were just little cowards ... adorable but still cowards. No one stood up to him like she did.

"You know what you did!" she fumed.

"I usually do, but what have I done to upset you, my dear?"

He sat with his eyes focused on her pacing. This was going to take some time ... so he propped his chin on his laced fingers and observed the tantrum.

"You didn't know I got married . Did you?"

"What are you talking about?" he looked mortified.

"You had him come and seduce me and propose! Just to seal the deal with his family! Didn't you? How much did you pay him? I should have known! I was so much in love with him that I could not see it … UNTIL they walked in. And she announced that YOU had just bought their company?"

He knew better than interrupting. Now he was in shock.

He had paled, "What on earth are you talking about my dear Adriana?"

"The Smith Oil Company. Does it ring a bell?" she stared at him with a … I dare you to deny it look … her hands on her hips. That's what he did when he got mad. She had her father's mannerisms. He was getting madder by the minute.

"What is the man's name in question?" he must be sure that every ounce of her tirade was false, before he could swat on her behind. He loved his daughter and could see she was genuinely hurting.

"Unitus de Pommel" she said as a matter-of-fact.

"Have a seat dear," pointing to the chair of leather with claw carved wooden legs. The same chair he always sat her in to talk. Through the years, he had referred to it as the hot seat!

"I prefer to stand, father," she spouted.

He stood and pointed to the chair that was offered.

"I said SIT Adriana! You maybe able to hear me better!"

He knew his blood pressure was up. He hated confrontations that is why he avoided them. She sat and crossed her arms, like a wee little tot that he had seen before. Heaven forbid! If she poked that lip out which she did not this time, maybe that is the one gesture she has out grown.

He paced in front of her.

"You got married and did not tell your own father. Then you accuse me of the unspeakable. I would never hire any man to deflower my daughter. Let alone pay him to do it! Not even for a business deal! Just what kind of a father do you think I am? Don't you dare say a word … young lady. You have hurt me deeply. I have no idea who this Unitus is. The deal I made was with a dear friend of mine named Trevor and his wife. She was a Smith married to my best friend named Samuel Smith. They do not and have never had a relative by the name of Unitus. I know that Bruce is Madeline's only son and he's married to a woman named Jana. Trevor has no children. You married a man that loves you … not because of me! Is that clear Adriana?"

"You are not kidding me … daddy?" She was crying and she never cried. He was holding her.

"NO, I never kid you my beautiful daughter. It is true I am a lowlife on most deals, but they do not affect my family in anyway. NEVER has, and I don't intend to start now."

"Daddy I have made a grave mistake then … how can I ever make it right?" Adriana asked.

"You go to him and tell him you have made a mistake! Simple as that. If he has any sense in his head, he will forgive you! You must bring him to meet me."

"I will daddy! I have a plane to catch!" Adriana kissed him and began running out of the building while dialing numbers to the airport.

By the time she got to Hendersonville, Unitus was gone.

He could not stay in that house so he left earlier than planned. All the pictures in that old house, were of a happy family and they were plastered on every wall.

He hopped a red eye flight straight to Washington, DC and got a taxi to Langley Field. They would be congratulating him on his marriage and he was prepared for it overtly, but his insides were churning at the mention of marriage.

He had no regrets … she was still everything he had ever wanted. He would do it all again the same way. She would want a quickie divorce, but he promised himself that she would have to see him first before he would give his signature.

Roscoe met with the Social Worker named Janie Andrews. She reported Debbie … Tate's girl friend that had been assaulted … was adjusting fairly well to the battered shelter. Trevor was with Roscoe. They were introduced and Trevor told her of his detective credentials. Andrews said, "That is great … we need all the help that we can get!"

"You know our funds are limited," she stated.

"I'll work for nothing on this one," Trevor assured her.

"Nothing is okay by me!" Janie laid it all out on the table.

"The price is right," Janie said again elated she had help.

"When can I get started, Roscoe is kind of tied up with his newborn twins right now?" Trevor informed her.

"I have a list that we are to follow to the letter," Janie pulled it from the back of her clipboard and handed Trevor a copy.

"We will need anyone with power … to go up against the school system. It will be worth it. This poor child needs our support. I am going to call many of my colleagues to help also. I believe with Roscoe, you, and I, we will make a positive impact on the outcome. Thank you again, Mr. Porter." She shook his and Roscoe's hand and she was off to her next client.

Roscoe looked at Trevor, "Those kids don't stand a chance unless we help!"

Trevor admitted, "I agree. Those punks don't know who they are up against. We must remain low key though, so the school does not get a whiff of our involvement, otherwise they will send out their BIG dogs."

Roscoe said reluctantly, "I agree."

Madeline was anxious for Trevor's return. He was her hero. He walked into the room and she was still in her blue negligee. His eyebrows furrowed, "Are you expecting the milkman, darling?"

"No actually, I was panting after the mailman!" she stood and added, "He has just arrived!"

He took her in his arms and whispered, "I do have a special delivery for Mrs. Trevor Porter."

"I am her," kissing him with arms around his neck and a leg wrapped around his thigh. She said, "that would be the package I ordered."

"We finally are alone. Would you like to unwrap it here, or in our bedroom my dear?"

She licked his ear and replied in a purr, "Away from the maddening crowd that may appear any minute."

He scooped her up and made it a few steps, "Let's go to the cabana and we can have a leisurely swim afterward?"

"You read my mind!" Madeline had the best man ever. He was her equal. She had loved Sam her deceased husband who died in the plane crash, but he could never bring out the passion in her that Trevor did. They made wild passionate love and swam as the night drew nigh.

The bear had given them a scare and an electric fence had been installed to protect the dogs. Soon the horses would arrive, and Trevor wanted the grand kids and great kids to enjoy riding. They would be able to ride along the mountain trails and fish in the streams as well as off the boat dock. These plans fit well into the future of these three baby boys.

"Until the babies are older, we grownups can enjoy. Bruce can teach Jana to ride," Trevor told Madeline as they sat by the pool watching the sun set.

"There are three boys already that you can teach to ride!" she said.

"Who?" Trevor asked.

"Bruce, Roscoe, and Guy ... I never had time to teach them. So you have a big job, now!"

"You mean Sam never taught Bruce to ride a horse?" Trevor looked in shock. "A Texan not know how to ride? My! My!"

"Nope ... he was too busy working ... and then the plane crash," she sighed.

"Well he shall learn with Jana, soon as the horses get here. If Guy and Roscoe don't know how to ride, then Kyleigh and Beatrice don't either. Am I right?"

"You are the leader of this pack?" she nodded her head.

"Yes! You are right, my love," Madeline teased.

"You are gonna have your hands full," she added smiling.

"Sounds like I need to get on the horn, and have at least two more horses added, and a couple of experts to help me train my boys and girls?" he was grinning.

She said, "Life was so much simpler for you until I came back into your life."

"Yes ... but I would not change a thing. I love our family warts and all!" Trevor kissed her hand and held on tight as she laid her head on his shoulder.

"You haven't told me about how it went with the TEENS Roscoe is helping?"

"I'll tell you tomorrow. I want us to just enjoy tonight. The beautiful moon reflecting over the lake. It is so peaceful here!"

Then they saw a car speeding down their road … doing at least a hundred …

CHAPTER THREE

The car slammed on brakes and out jumps Adriana. She runs up to the house, and starts ringing the doorbell nonstop, and pounding on the door like a madwoman.

"Where is he? Where is he?" she was hysterically crying his name …"Where is Unitus? I have made such a MISTAKE FORGIVE me!" She thought he was inside where she had left him last. She hoped he was in this house. "Please be here!"

Madeline opened the door and put her arms around her. "Calm down, my dear. We all make mistakes … Now! Now! Catch your breath and let's get you something to drink. Trevor can you get something to calm her nerves!"

Madeline said, "Let's go in the house and we can find out where Unitus is." She walked with her to the den. She was trembling and still sobbing.

"Thank you! I just need to see him tonight!" Adriana wailed.

"Okay, we will call Roscoe and see where he is. OK? He took him to my old house earlier this week," GM said.

"Thank you so much. I have been such a fool!" sipping the brandy Trevor had given her which seem to be calming her.

"Roscoe where might Unitus be? Still at my home in the city?" Madeline asked.

"No ma'am, he left yesterday for DC. Why?" Roscoe asked.

"Adriana has come back to apologize. She loves him so much. She is in with Trevor crying her eyes out. Poor child knows she is now HUMAN. People make mistakes. Can you call him and tell him, she is here."

"I think Bruce may have better luck! I will call him at Guy's. They are still playing with the baby. Talk later!" Roscoe hung up.

Madeline came back in the den and sat by Adriana.

"Roscoe is going to get Bruce to find out where he is. You don't worry, they will find him."

"They can't find him! He sent me a letter that he was going to his next assignment and that I would not be able to break the code. He knew I was wrong. Why didn't he come after me Madeline? Why?"

"Sometimes men can hurt ... and don't know what to say. Unitus has always been Bruce's friend. I have not been around my son in five years because I made a mistake. I believed the wrong person, I thought he helped kill his father. ... Dear Adriana, I had to admit to my son ... how wrong I was! Now we have forgiven each other as you and Unitus will. I can see you both love each other deeply."

Adriana was asleep on the sofa when Bruce and Jana returned. She jumped up, "Did you find him Bruce? Please tell me you found him," pleading with her eyes.

"No, Adriana! I have tried. He has gone to fulfill his duty to the agency. He cannot make any contact with me or his life would be in danger. He will contact me when he can. If and when, he does ... you will be the first to know.

I have never seen him this broken, but when he learns you came back he will rejoice. You do realize he loves you with every ounce of his being?"

She was numb and lifeless. Barely able to speak, "I know he does NOW that I have spoken to my father. He told me he would never use me to make a deal. So I was wrong on both counts. I am a loser. I have lost the only man ... I have ever loved. He told me how smart I was. Book wise, I have excelled ... yes! But now I feel so so stupid!"

She was pacing and flipping her hair the way Unitus liked her to do, then continued. "I have never let a man get close to me. Unitus was my first love LOL and my last! I will love him to the day I die. I must go home now. I have bothered you good people long enough."

"Nonsense you can stay as long as you want to my dear!"

"I have to go home and back to work. That is the best thing for me, is to work until I hear from Bruce." Jana hugged her and said, "Stay the night!"

"I can't. The last night I spent with him was here! I can't stay. You do understand? Call me a cab, PLEASE," she walked to the door to stare at the moon and the mountains. "He loved it here and I now ... I see why!" she paused.

"You people are his family. He wanted me to meet his family. His beautiful family. I have never had a family. It was always nannies and maids and never a mother of any of my father's many wives loved me. They just tolerated me. I don't know why I am talking so much, it must be the brandy. At least, I am going to blame it on the brandy!" The taxi was there, each family member hugged her saying, "We love you."

Guy and Kyleigh had settled little Madison in for the night, and Guy was feeling frisky. He picked Kyleigh up and spun her around. She was trying not to giggle, but he was so horny and it had been such a long time.

He was leaving it up to her, "Have your way with me woman!" Her eyes were dancing and her hands were roaming in all the right places.

He said, "Are you sure?"

She said, "Yes! It has been forty days since the C-section."

He was shaking his head, "Don't do that … I cannot take it! Stop unless I can have you! It had been nearly TWO months!

She said, "You can always have me. You just have to go slow and slower than you ever have. That's all!" Kyleigh said.

"Oh my goodness!" He was in and not moving. "Oh that feels so good. Don't move Kyleigh, I will hurt you."

"You can never hurt me. My stitches have healed nicely. You just hold your breath till I'm done."

"You are killing me!" he began trembling.

"OH yes that's like my vibrator … Oh babe … slow down," she cooed. "It is good go slow!" she was almost screaming and she thought of the dog.

He had to admit going slow intensified every tiny nerve ending. They were coming unraveled …wave after wave. He barely moved and it went on and on.

"Kyleigh!" You are awesome. You teach me something new every time that I did not think I could do. Just don't move. Sh... here it comes again!"

She said, "I will have mercy... mercy." Then she was trembling and erupting. "I have missed you so much!"

"Kyleigh don't! Please I swore I would never hurt you! Neveeeer!"

"Guy! You have to please, do it! Pleaseeeee now!" and he did. They were both gasping for air.

They lay there. Neither wanting to move to see the damage them may had done. He picked her up and took her to the shower and they showered and they both changed the bed.

She looked at him and said, "When we work together, we can do anything." He kissed her until she was breathless again.

He had to be the sensible one, "We better not push it!"

"You are right!" but she was under the covers loving him again.

She said, "I just want you to be completely satisfied."

"I am totally satisfied. I have been since the day we got married. I never want to do it without you, okay?" Guy stated.

"Okay, understood. So when do you think you can love me slow again?" she purred.

"Tomorrow night?" she asked with a wink.

"It's a date little wifey of mine. God your boobs are huge. Can we keep them!" Guy begged.

She swatted him, "No, they are Madison's."

"He'll be awake in a few …" Guy said.

"When he goes to sleep, I may jump your bones mister! If you don't stop …" Kyleigh grinned.

Beatrice and Roscoe were not having as good a time because when one baby was asleep, then the other was awake. Which was fine during the day, Beatrice could manage. She was not breastfeeding, but using the pump. With two it meant the babies, both got the same amount of milk.

Roscoe enjoyed feeding his boys. The one with the mole under his left ear was Caleb, and Cain had a strawberry on his right butt cheek.

"Now no one can say, I don't know which is which," Roscoe was muttering as he was changing Strawberry's diaper … oops I mean Cain's diaper," smiling at Beatrice as she was feeding Caleb.

"They will both be asleep in an hour. You want to hanky panky?" Beatrice was asking Roscoe.

He pointed his finger at himself, "Are you talking to me?Not tonight Dear," shaking his head.

Beatrice wiggled up behind him and grabbed him, "Are you sure?" staring into his eyes.

He turned and looked at her, "Not tonight Dear!"

Beatrice said, "Okay … who's the slut that has moved into town?"

"No one has moved in that I know of … I have a wife that would make chop liver out of me, if I even whistle at a slutty slut slut … Do you know my wife? She has the biggest..."

Roscoe eyebrows were going up and down … "Appetite!" he grinned at her.

She said, "And don't you ever forget it buster," they had no stitches to worry about. The boys were asleep and Roscoe was loving his wife to sleep. "I love the way you cup my mouth while I …. I know it is to keeps that dog from biting your ass, but it is a real erotic feeling. Do it again!"

"Woman … stop talking and let's get it on" and he slapped her butt good.

Falling into the great abyss. He jumped off the bed, "Beatrice honey! Darling! The love of my life! Do you think you could get pregnant this early since you are not on the pill yet?" Roscoe needed to know this right now. This very minute.

"OF course, I can. It happens all the time. Only we could have TRIPLETS this time because dang my orgasms are three times better than they were before the twins. Oh baby!"

He nearly fainted. "Tell me you are joking?"

She lay in bed, wiggling her index finger to come hither to her, "Come to mama! We have one more hour and all will be gone, dry up, and packed away till next week!"

Roscoe was running and dove into the bed, "Thanks for reminding me. I'd love triplets with you, darling! Let's make them tonight! Yep, got to have me some more more babies!"

"Roscoe, honey ... don't scream you will wake up the dog and he'll bite your tushy!" Beatrice smiled.

He helped her feed the twins before going to work. Kissing her red hair and said, "You were fabulous last night. If the triplets need anything, just give me a call."

She blew him a kiss, "Of course, I will ghostbuster. Love you big guy!"

Roscoe wanted to stop by the library this afternoon to see Tate. He was there waiting.

"How is she, Roscoe? I gotta know?" Tate was trying not to talk loud, but he was so anxious. He couldn't help it.

"I talked to Janie the Social Worker and she says she is adjusting. It is hard on anyone in a new surrounding. Write her a letter and I will deliver it! That way no phone calls that can be overheard or traced. The school atmosphere, no bullies hanging with you, Tate?" Roscoe said looking at Tate.

Tate would not make eye contact, "It's the same old, same old. I don't let it bother me, Man. My only concern is doing my classwork and knowing Debbie is SAFE."

The team had squared him in a corner and asked him where she was? They almost broke his arm, but he told them, "I don't give a sh... where she is.! I ain't her keeper you frigging jocks. Bite my ass!" and they fell for it and let go.

If he told Roscoe he would put pressure on them and they would know it was because of him. The jocks visit the library to check out chicks to do their homework. If they see Roscoe and I talking, they are going to beat me down, he told himself.

"Your security building … is it open day and night? If I need help … can I go there?" Tate asked.

"OF course you can and they can call me anytime day or night!" Roscoe fist bumped him and Tate was gone.

Coraine met Tate at the laundry door at Aunt Eunice's.

"You been messing with my friend Debbie. I know she had the hots for you, so where is she? You didn't kill her, did you?" his cousin was high as a Georgia pine. He had to get her to talk.

"I haven't seen her this week!" that was the truth.

"What's up with you? Coraine how can I help you?" He looked into her eyes. She was stoned.

"You can't help me. Nobody can! I am too far gone! She told you, didn't she? The little whore!" She was angry at Debbie, but would not rat her only friend out. She knew, he had helped Debbie.

The football team could f--- her up some more, but she would never tell them, even if they killed her. She would never tell. She had made up her mind up to take as much of any kind of drug or drugs that would numb her pain. Make the voices stop. The voices of the team grunting and visions of them raping her that went on forever. "All SEVEN of those bastards, I wish would burn in hell for what they did to Debbie and me!"

"Can't you see that you need to get help? How about us going over to the drug rehab center. You are my cousin.

Your mom has no clue what is wrong with you? I can only imagine what has happened to you, but drugs are not the answer."

"Maybe! Maybe I will," she said. Tate was trying to get her to see that. Then in walks Aunt Eunice, and Coraine gives her mom the middle finger and out the door, she went.

That's the last time he saw Coraine. She had not been home in four days and his aunt was freaking out.

"I got to go to the police station and file a missing person report on her. Tate can you watch the boys?" The police told her that they had found Coraine in a ditch two days before, but she had no identification on her.

Aunt Eunice identified the body and went to the funeral home, all while he is doing homework and watching the boys.

When his aunt came in, she told everyone and he ran to the library to see Roscoe, but he wasn't there. So he went to the security building and grabbed and hugged Roscoe.

Roscoe took him into his office.

He told Roscoe what Coraine had told him that the team was after her again and if they got her, she would take all the drugs she could get.

"Roscoe can they get sperm out of her. I've seen on TV that DNA can convict people. She told me, it was seven of them. So there should be seven DNA stuff." He was so distraught that he repeated himself. "She would not go get help! I tried to take her ... She told me, if they DID NOT MESS with her that she would think about rehab ......"

"I know you did. You tried," Roscoe said.

"Debbie will hear so I wrote her a note. To please not leave that place. Roscoe I am so afraid, they will find her. There are always snitches in places like that. Can you take her to another state till this is over? I can't think about her and help my aunt at the same time. PLEASE! I'll tell you now they have been after me asking about her, but I didn't tell them anything!" He finally showed Roscoe … his bruises had blackened and there were more than Roscoe could record. So he took pictures with his cell phone and stored them as evidence.

"I will put two men on tonight to protect your home, and if your aunt needs anything let me know?"

"She needs a casket," and Tate walked out and went home.

Roscoe got Trevor on the phone and asked him to met him at Guy's and to bring Bruce. He told Beatrice to call Madeline and Jana, if she needed anything that they would be working through the night.

Madeline was furious that they would not let her help.

Then she realized she was needed worse to help look after the women and babies more while the men worked on this case.

"The men are right for once," she said to herself.

"You 'all can use GM & GS Private Investigation Service office, instead of Guy's house. I will stay with Kyleigh. Now go, get!" Madeline was a worrier though.

This is like nothing she had ever handled. The school had always had a good reputation. So wonder what went wrong? That she would like to know, because eventually these three great grandsons would be going to THAT school."

CHAPTER FOUR

Debbie was watching the TV when she saw Coraine's picture splashed across the screen. The caption was sixteen year old dies of drug overdose.

She saw reporters around Coraine's house trying to get interviews with the family. Coraine's mother swatted at the camera crew. "Why don't you leeches go away!" hugging her nine year old son Jason who was crying, and the thirteen year old skateboarder son Corey had his arms around both of them.

Where was Tate? Debbie had a teardrop running down her face, but no sounds came out of her mouth. Then Roscoe came through the door followed by a white haired man.

She ran and hugged Roscoe, "Where is Tate? They will kill him. Help me! Please. They will find this place!" she was so pale and trembling uncontrollably.

Roscoe hugged her and introduced her to his grandfather, Trevor. Who also hugged her. "Everything is going to be all right. We are going to get you another place to stay. Don't you worry little girl … you are going to be safe!"

The SBI had been brought in and Trevor had reviewed with them the severity of the situation. They agreed. The medical examiner was made aware of the request for toxicology and DNA to be done and crime investigators would take hair samples and clothing samples, etc. They were reporting possible homicide instead of a suicide. All evidence needed to be obtained before it could be tampered with. Trevor told them of the gang rape and the need to protect Debbie who would be a star witness. The witness protection team was summoned and she was whisk away to a safe house where there would be 24hours/7days a week staff guarding her.

When she arrived, there sat Tate. She ran to him. "I am so glad that they are going to protect both of us. They would have killed you to find out where I was ..." Debbie sighed.

Roscoe was behind her, and Tate grabbed him and hugged him. "It's going to be alright, kids. You two just have to stay put!!! There is a female guard that you, Debbie can go to if you need anything, and Tate two male guards will be here around the clock. You have my cell number. This is going to take awhile. You both may have to be moved again."

Roscoe was pacing and Trevor was nodding his head. "There are seven families' that sons may be prosecuted. So we know, they will not sit and let their boys go to jail. If they can help it! I hate to ask you two, but I have to have a list of the seven boys' names. While you are writing, I will be speaking to the guards and SBI."

Trevor could see Roscoe was dealing well professionally with this painful situation, but there was something else Roscoe was not saying. He needed to find out.

"Okay Son! What is it? Unload," staring at Roscoe who was now sitting in the police car and appeared to be stunned.

"Roscoe ... What is it?" Trevor was getting worried.

"Inscoe just told me something that I had no idea about until now … Tate's last name is Shackleford. GRANDMA is going to freak out. Inscoe said, "His brother is Adam Shackleford and GUY is going to freak out." He looked at Trevor and shook his head from side to side.

"How can such a sweet kid be KIN to such monsters? Tell me what to do?" He placed his head on the steering wheel.

"Oh wise one... Tell me what to do? I have to protect these two kids. They are sitting ducks. They will be slaughtered by those uppety parents and the real real monsters are those creepy little rich kids that think the world owes them everything … and they can do anything, and their parents will get them out of it! They think they are above the law!"

"Not this time … Not this time Roscoe!" Trevor was eyeballing his longtime friend Dwight Howell who was in the Crime Lab Department. He had been on the Dallas-Fort Worth area division before transferring here.

"Small world … Dwight," shaking his hand. "Glad to see you. Did you by any chance hear what my grandson said?"

"Affirmative Trevor. Good to see you, too. I heard Roscoe was on the police force before opening his Security Business," Dwight replied.

"Yep … You always do your homework! He has been advising and helping to get this girl into a battered shelter. The boy has been beaten up by the same gang that hurt the girl. What do you think, we should do first?" in the past Dwight had always like to be in charge of everything so why not let him now.

"You take Roscoe on home and leave it to me. We will take care of them and talk to you tomorrow!" he instructed.

"Thanks Dwight. I appreciate it!"

On the way home Trevor told Roscoe, "That is the right man for this job."

"Why are you saying it like that … your face is all smiles … Give?" Roscoe asked.

"His niece was raped by a college student and he lowered the BOOM on him, and got enough evidence to put him away … I just hope he does the same here!"

"Can we tell Grandma and Guy together about Tate?" Roscoe was asking without pleading.

Trevor said, "For you, I will," and gave Roscoe a hug.

"I will withhold that information from her until you come over tomorrow with Guy. All else I need to tell her, so her wheels will stop turning. She will know it is being handled by the best. Goodnight, son!" Roscoe got out of the car and went in to see his wife and babies.

Debbie was still in Tate's arms. She had not moved for two hours. Just staring into space. He did not know what to say.

He was deep in thought about his aunt Eunice and the kids.

When this was all over, he and Debbie would put the most beautiful flowers on Coraine's grave.

He would not be allowed to leave for any reason nor would Debbie. She had no more tears. They had fell without any sobbing. She looked numb.

He asked, "Are you hungry?"

"No, are you?" Debbie said.

Tate stretched his arm that had gone to sleep, "The woman cop said we needed to eat so we wouldn't get sick. That we would need our strength in the days to come. I guess she is right."

They both ate the candy bars and drank the sodas in front of them. All else they left on their trays.

Bruce and Jana were sitting with Madeline by the fireplace when Trevor came in and hung his coat up.

"Any sign of that bear?" Trevor had six eyes wanting to know what had been happening and the bear could wait.

He told them all except about Tate. Madeline was relieved when she heard the SBI was staying.

The SBI was using GM & GS Private Investigation Service as their home base since this was a small town, and they had used it before on the Chris Shackleford case.

The motels were full so they were staying at Madeline's old home. Trevor had insisted. They knew the layout.

Trevor could hardly look Madeline in the eyes and she knew there was something else that he was not telling her, but he looked dog-tired. She would let him be for tonight.

Unitus and Barry had been sent to Miami to intermingle with the drug trafficking operations and they were incognito.

Unitus could speak Portuguese, Spanish, and Japanese.

He was informed about the suspected shipment from Japan that had not arrived. One of the Spaniards said, "It's nada!"

Barry Turner was a pilot, but he also often went undercover to back up Unitus. He was fluent in Japanese and said "MAO JUNG gonna be very angry?" Three men with knives drawn rushed to him.

Unitus intervened, "What's the problem?"

One was speaking "NEVER say that name again imbecile."

He took his index finger and slid it across his throat area, "Or you dead!"

Barry cowered behind Unitus who was shaking his head, "He's a manequim" and they roared laughing.

Barry is shaking his head affirmatively, "Yes I am a dummy!"

Then the whole crew at the wharf were laughing as they continued their manual labor, BUT Unitus knew it was not going to be easy for them to ever leave this pier alive.

He had gone online before he left Hendersonville and downloaded a picture of Adriana and had it in his chest pocket. It was laminated, so that it would withstand the sweat and filth that he was working around today. He reached into his pocket.

The foreman rushed to see what he had. He snatched the picture out of Unitus's hand. Unitus furrowed his brow and his nostrils were flared, and he said, "Minha garota!"

Then he did the unthinkable, he snatched the picture back. The crew gasped. Unitus said, "MY GIRL!"

The foreman laughed so hard, he spoke English and said, "NO WAY IN HELL IS THAT YOUR GIRL!"

Unitus broke out in a grin and spoke in English, "You are so right, but I can dream!"

The foreman said, "Dream on loser!"

Barry climbed out from under a barrel that he had hid in, "You amaze me! That was a good distraction. I might try that sometime," Barry grinned.

Unitus told him, "Make sure I am not around when you do! Because only rats get under barrels."

Barry said to one of the crew, "I think he is really pissed at me." They were shaking their heads like we don't know what you are saying.

Unitus really missed Bruce. Bruce always had his back from this day forward no one is watching mine, but me. He was going into Bruce mode. Sleeping ten minutes out of every hour around the clock.

They were housed in the blighted neighborhood and the morning seemed, it would never come. Unitus had his contact but Barry was a pain in the neck. Barry said, "I'm not going to make it through this one."

"We have to get the job done at all cost. You can go if you want to, but I nor no one else would be able to find you. Best you stick with me, little buddy," Unitus told him.

"I am not Bruce so don't you expect it … I will set the fuse and then you get out! You hear me I can't look back! The coast guard will pick us up … then I'll fly us back. Okay?"

"Sounds good … Don't look back!"

Their mission went down and the barrels that had cocaine in them were brought in from Japan and from Mao Jung. This bomb they set would blow up their operation and that was their only objective. To disrupt and leave the rest up to the Coast Guard, and Military, and DEA agents.

As they were coming out of the hold, Barry ran zigzag as did Unitus, but that foreman had an eye on Unitus.

When the side of the ship blew, the foreman went after Unitus and blew a hole in his leg with a grenade. He fell and that was all he remembered, until he woke up at Walter Reed National Military Hospital. The military had saved his life by emergency care within minutes and transported him within twenty two hours to the warrior wound care floor.

He had lost his RIGHT lower leg and was transported to the Amputee Rehab center where he would stay at least six months or longer if need be.

He was a warrior and would advance quickly. He was the type of man that pushed himself to be the best that he could be. Bruce and Jana came to visit. He was told by them about Adriana coming to find him the week that he left.

"Yes, she loves you with all her heart. She had been to see her father, and he told her the truth. She said she felt like an idiot and had to apologize to you Unitus. She truly loves you," Jana was pleading for him to see her.

Bruce said, "I was there I saw her. Man I wouldn't lie to you. She loves you."

Unitus had not spoken. Then he turned to look out the window in his wheelchair and said, "she loves the man that ... I once was."

"Unitus you are a dumb ass, if you don't give your wife the choice. At least see the woman. Come to the ranch with us! Adriana got me another six month extension. I want you to visit and stay in Hendersonville. Live near your family!" Bruce pleaded.

"We are your family Unitus. Come home with us," Jana kissed him on the cheek.

"Bruce you know that Barry DIDN'T make it! I was suppose to protect him. That could have been you. If you promise me Bruce that you will NOT accept any more missions, then I will go to Hendersonville. I cannot lose another friend," Unitus was looking up at Bruce.

"It's a deal ... I'm here for you ... always," Bruce hugged him and Jana was crying because her husband was not going back into harms way either.

"Both of you have made me so happy," Jana was making plans and the men were packing Unitus's supplies and anticipating his needs for travel.

"Trevor sent us in his plane so the flight should be smooth."

Bruce was relieved his friend actually was coming home. He had his prosthesis on and had learned to use it, but when traveling the wheelchair would be easier on him. It was electric and he would have time to learn all the ways his new leg worked in the real world when they got home.

Jana was down the hall talking to Adriana on the phone. She had begged to see him all this time that he had been at Walter Reed, but he would not allow her a visit.

He told Jana, "If and when I see her, I will be standing."

He could stand now and walk very well. He had just been so depressed about poor Barry. He had to snap out of it.

Jana had asked her if SHE wanted to see him.

"I have begged for so long, do you have to ask?" Adriana stated.

"I ask you to be there way before we get there, and stay with Madeline. She can give you advice and help you ready yourself for him. He still is fragile, but tries to put on a good face. He made a statement that you were in love with the man that he once WAS. It will be your job to convince him that you are in love with him ... period. Are you sure about your feelings for him?" Jana asked.

"Yes positive!" Adriana said.

"We'll see you soon then. Text me if you need me," Jana hung up and jumped for joy and people were staring. The little five foot woman was making a scene as her husband came around the corner. Unitus was driving his wheels and they were off to the airport.

CHAPTER FIVE

Beatrice looked at her seven month old twins and said "You guys are wearing on my back. It's about time for them to start walking." She sipped her coffee and looked at her husband who was holding his back and limping to the kitchen chair.

"You are mocking me! True I want them to get out of the way for our next two. You heard what the doctor said," smiling and raising two fingers ... waving them at him.

He pretended a jack knife dive to the floor and the boys laughed hysterically at their father.

"You predicted this! You wanted to make my dreams come true. A baseball team of my very own!" he kissed her hand. As the twins threw cereal at their parents who had began smooching in the breakfast nook.

Beatrice said after she got her breath, "Don't you think they are a little young to watch x-rated movies in the kitchen?"

"Nah ... I think they've been desensitized to our amorous adventures by now," grinning at his half naked wife. She liked to remain sexy for her big guy and the lacy getup was turning him on.

"Okay you are asking for it?" she winked at him.

"You bet I am," he was panting like a dog.

She grabbed the twins and said, "Go to work and I will slip into something more comfortable tonight!" she let her strap fall off one arm and the boys were wiggling so they kicked the rest off. On the way to bathroom, "got to give the boys a bath," she said.

"I wanna take a bath," he said with puppy dog eyes.

"Go … don't touch … or you will be terribly late for work!"

"Good point ... kiss kiss ... see you tonight!" out the door he went at a running pace.

He had been working on Tate's case nonstop and it was finally settled when the trial would begin. The teenagers, Tate and Debbie were still in the witness protection program and they were excelling in their studies. Tate had been able to get Debbie interested in her schoolwork. The social worker had praised her. The more praise she and Roscoe gave her, the more Debbie had dug in and brought her grades up.

This had been a labor of love for Trevor. Roscoe was deeply thankful, he had come into his grandma's life. It is no telling what would have happened to these teens, if he hadn't. He had his hands full with the twins, so everyday he could not go to check on them, Trevor was there.

Trevor said one day to Roscoe, "There is no doubt this young man Tate, is not of the same mold, as his father and brother. He is a good kid."

Roscoe said, "Yeah, he is! That's what they told GM that I was a good kid, and she took me in. I'm just paying it forward. She adjusted after I told her this. Grandma softened right up after that initial shock we gave her. Didn't she?"

"Yes... it was a shock for her. She said it was the name that she could not get pass ... the kid's last name. How about we ADOPT him Trev?"

"I told her I was too old to have children," Trevor looked at Roscoe and winked.

"But I now see that you can conceive at any age. TATE ALEXANDER PORTER does have a nice ring. I am glad your grandma did not have to go through with that natural child birth at her age. That I could NOT have survived!" and they both laughed.

Trevor patted Roscoe on the back, "Congrats I hear you are going to have twins. I hope this time it will be girls."

"Thanks, me too. They can be tomboys and play ball, if they so choose." Roscoe was still dreaming of his own baseball team when the door slammed.

"My cue to get the ball rolling. See ya!" Roscoe drove off.

"It's about time you got here. The sheriff was going to send out a posse," ... Roscoe's secretary said.

"I was only fifteen minutes late," Roscoe said and rushed around her into his office.

"And hour and fifteen minutes late, boss ... But who's counting?" She began with one finger after the other to count, "The prosecutor, the DA, Judge Bernie, the Parents!"

"Alright! Alright! So I'm a few minutes late," he pointed to her. "But I have this wonderful and beautiful secretary that goes to bat for her boss ... when he tarries!" Roscoe gave her a big grin.

"You betcha and don't you forget it when you write my paycheck!" she blushed and added, "Beautiful! Wonderful!" fluffing her short pixie hair cut. "That's my bonus, forget the money. Just keep those words coming my way honey, and I will work for you forever." She began typing as fast as she could.

He closed the door and said, "I know Freda. I know you will!"

The intercom blared, "I heard that!" Freda said.

"Of course, you did. You hear everything in this office!" click and he cut off the intercom.

"Oh crap!" rubbing his forehead retracing Beatrice's steps this week. Had she been to his office. Why yes, I do believe she has! He began frowning and wondering, if he had cut the intercom off that day.

"I'm losing my own security when it comes to my wife. She has messed my …. up!"

Fumbling through his papers, he found the materials he needed for court. Reviewing them over and over for errors until he knew, they were perfect. Just what his clients needed and the evidence he had guarded for so long. Roscoe breathed a sigh of relief.

Madeline had gone to see Madison who immediately held out his arms for his "NANA."

"How are you today my darling?" Madeline asked.

"I'm doing okay and we do appreciate you coming and babysitting for us!" Kyleigh kissed her on the cheek and flew out the door with her husband who was taking her to see her doctor.

"I had rather go have my teeth pulled than go see him, but you say my doctor is wonderful. Are you sure you don't want to just go and fool around in the woods somewhere?"

Kyleigh could see Guy closing his eyes and digesting what his senses were doing to his inner self. He did not pull off the road this time as he did last month and cancel her appoint-ment in a matter of seconds.

"I must be losing my touch!" and she proceeded to test her tactile qualities. He had grabbed her hand.

"It won't work. I am going to get you there today come hell or high waters!" he drove a little faster.

"Are you sure? You are the best medicine and the only dosage I need is right here!" she had slipped her tiny hand in his trouser pocket. He decided he'd show her that no matter how much she tried he was going to … going to …

"Sit up darling. You are making people stare," Guy said.

"Why haven't they ever had their zipper licked?" she got out and slammed the door.

She had her pre- pregnancy body back and it was doing a number on him. She was bouncing those perky little breasts as she walked in her three inch heels. Her derriere was firm and hugged by her tight slim skirt that had a slit up front.

"What was I thinking? Stop this elevator now!" he did.

She said, "Put that thing away! I have a doctor's appointment! You want me to go so I will go!" she is talking fast … all the while he had raised her skirt and took her lacy panties and put them neatly in her purse. He placed her legs around him while she was still talking and …....ecstasy!

The plane had touched down at the Charlotte Airport, Bruce was calling for James to bring the white limo out to the plane. Unitus had slept most of the way and Jana knew it was so he would not have to talk.

The car was loaded and they were driving up the long road with the white fence. The miles of fence like in Dallas.

Unitus said, "This is so weird. It feels like the same road as in Dallas. I remember every winding bend that Adriana and I took to get here. It is so beautiful. Thank you Bruce for having my back. You knew I would not come on my own. I am glad I did."

"I knew... Always this is your home," and Bruce patted Jana's thigh and grabbed her hand and squeezed it.

Unitus had a pit in his stomach when he saw the house. This house was where he had brought his brand new bride. The same house she had ran out of crying, vowing to never speak to him again. Never to forgive him.

They had all the wheelchair assembled and Unitus transferred into it and he wanted to look around before going inside.

"It's been a long time since I breathed fresh air!" he inhaled and looked at Bruce who was kicking a rock.

"What's wrong with you?" Unitus asked.

"There is a surprise party inside ... my mother and Trevor have been planning all week ... I am pulled to do what you want to do ... and I am pulled to not disappoint them. What you say we go in?" Unitus nodded and rolled up to the door.

Jana opened the door and he rolled in, followed by Bruce.

Bruce knew he had better stay by the door so Unitus wouldn't roll himself right back out. He knew his friend wanted to be standing when he saw her again.

This was Bruce's only fear that he would reject her from his low seat. He would help him with either way it could go.

There she stood in a gorgeous simple sheath of gold. Hair flipped to one side like he liked it. No makeup... no high heels ... just comfortable sandals.

41

His ring was still on her finger. It had a diamond that she loved and the wedding band was intact. His wedding ring had been cut off his finger before surgery and he had it in his suitcase, but it needed repair.

He closed his eyes. He thought he was dreaming only his mirage was walking toward him.

Her hips were swaying as he remembered. She was licking her lips as he remembered.

"Stop!" and he spoke into Bruce's his ear and they went out. Jana went out and Bruce whispered in her ear.

All else were stunned that they had left.

"He wants ten minutes," Jana said and winked.

The whole room let out a sigh. Jana hugged Adriana.

Bruce helped Unitus get his new leg out and he put it on and faced the mirror. He was standing tall as ever and he had changed to her favorite jeans and his cobalt blue Henley. He had had his new foot made to fit his snakeskin slip-on shoes and he was dressed as he was the first day at her gym.

When he walked in there was a gasp from Adriana, and she ran to him. She stood toe to toe with him. He had not stopped his weight training and he was able to lift her with ease to his height and hold her there, while he devoured her mouth in front of everyone. They decided to go into the dining room and feast, while Unitus and Adriana continued in the hallway.

"I love you so much Unitus. Promise me we will never be apart. Forgive me!" tears running down her cheeks as she held on to him with all her might.

She could feel him respond on her legs and she was breathing so rapidly or was that him.

"I love you too, my wife" and he buried his head in her neck and added. "We must go into that room over there before I do something exciting to you right here." He was staring into her eyes.

"I told you before I didn't care here, there or everywhere, but you are right it may embarrass our hosts. I'll get down."

"Don't you dare! Just open that door when I walk with you and that's all the help I need. Don't kiss me again till we are inside. Otherwise, I may forget where I am again."

"Okay!" and he walked slowly but she could feel him growing and she closed her eyes.

"OH MY GOD How you are doing it to me?" He kissed her quickly because they were inside the tiny bathroom.

"Shut the door Adriana honey! If you want to!" because he was not going to ever let her go again!

He was so strong and he wanted no help but she did anyway. She unzipped his jeans and she stepped out of her panties. Their reunion should have made the record in all the seismograph books. It moved the earth for them. As they climaxed, Adriana screamed and the dogs came running. Trevor caught them. Then after calming them. Unitus screamed or bellowed, the dogs went wild again. Bruce got the dogs that time. "They are going to hurt my dogs ears!" Trevor laughed.

After two hours, they emerged smiling. She had washed him and he had washed her, and then they could not help it. They had been apart for so long. They closed the door and did a repeat. "I have a surprise for you tonight Unitus! Don't touch! I've got a surprise for you too! But it can't wait for tonight!" He had her breast in his mouth and she said, "I need it now! Now!"

Three hours later they emerged and no one was around.

A note was on the refrigerator, "WE UNDERSTAND... FOOD INSIDE ... ENJOY!"

"We have the whole house to ourselves," Unitus said.

Adriana said, "No they have just gone to see the babies. By the time they get back, we will be long gone!"

"What are you talking about?" She had waited till he had ate. Then she walked around the table and kissed his tonsils.

"I have something to show you." They walked slowly to the backdoor. There was a ramp and beside it was a van. The door opened with a wheelchair lift. "I am going to ride in that wheelchair." She did ride him in the wheelchair and he maneuvered it to the van and she said, "I have to show you my place." His eyes were curious and his mouth stopped what he was doing.

"Run that by me again. Your place?" he asked.

Adriana's eyebrow went up and down, "Correction! OUR place! I got it encase my husband would take me back."

"You got to be kidding?" staring at her.

"We have been inside a tiny bathroom for how many hours and now you tell me this!" Unitus's eyes were bulging and the thoughts of her being in a bed like White Rock Lake came flashing back, was killing his libido. He sucked air in and blew it out. He shared his thoughts with her and now she was having flashbacks.

"We may never get this van up that hill!" She pointed up the mountain.

She had practiced driving it, "I'm driving!"

"As long as I get to drive tonight, I'll let you drive this van."

She drove them up to Roscoe's old bachelor pad that she had a contractor to put ramps and safety features in for Unitus to have ease whether walking or riding in the wheelchair.

He drove the wheelchair to the ramp and she jumped on straddling him.

"Do you won't to kill me … us?" Unitus asked.

"Are you complaining my love?" Adriana did the pouty lip everyone thought she had out grown.

"Not that!" he grinned. "I just might drive off the mountain because I lose my bearings around you. Always have!"

She grinned and got up, "Okay I see your point so I can ride you in the house then?"

"Of course!" The sunset was more spectacular on the mountainside this day. Unitus had removed his leg. He still had his knee and when they lay together she made him so happy. She kissed him everywhere to make him see she loved every inch of him.

From that day forward, he had no doubt whatsoever that this woman was his soul mate and lover forever. That she NEVER said what she DID NOT mean. He had wasted so much of their time. He would make it up to her.

"You know we have to apologize to the folks," he said.

"You may, but I'm not. They have known for sometime how crazy I am over you. I will stand beside you, if that's what you want to do!" she teased. She could not get enough of him.

"Leave the lights on all the time until I get use to this place." Really he just wanted to stare at her day and night until he could get the nightmares to go away. Replace them with visions of his wife doing everything.

"Can you cook?" he asked.

"Can you?" she asked.

"We may starve!" he stated.

"I am a slow learner!" he said.

"I know my love! So am I?"

"We can learn together!" she suggested.

"You'd make a good lawyer. You make a good case."

"I forgot to tell you I moved my practice here!"

Adding, "My first case is two abused teens named Tate and Debbie."

CHAPTER SIX

Tate was really having a problem and Debbie was really having a problem. They were emotionally a wreck, but they had a problem with normal biology. They couldn't keep their hands off each other. The TWELVE months were weighing on them being in close quarters, and at first Debbie was so indifferent and didn't respond at all to his advances. With no response, he had lost interest and he was respectful of her situation.

Then she did the unthinkable, he was in the shower and she joined him.

"Oh no! Trevor and Roscoe will kill me, and the guards will report it, and you might get pregnant, and it will be all over the newspapers."

"Shut up and kiss me!" she had her arms around his neck.

"We can feel each other! NOTHING else." She was rubbing his neck and he was rubbing her buttocks and nothing more.

"For the first time I feel alive." she said. He was soaping her.

"I am glad I was worried," he said. She was soaping him.

They were just talking as if they were doing their home-work.

"You know I have to stop!"

"I know I don't want you to."

"But yes you have to stop me!"

"When this is over we will see how we feel about each other, but until then. You and I have to stay far far far apart!"

"I understand. You don't want me!"

"Far from it … I want it to mean something to you."

"I want you. Until this minute, I didn't know it could be enjoyable. It has always been … painful and … awful."

He did not want to terrify her and she start screaming. They were kissing, and he jumped for the guard was in the room.

She had put pillows on her bed under the covers and it looked like she was asleep.

"You in there?" the female guard asked.

"Yeah taking a shower. I'll be out soon!" Tate said.

Debbie was kissing his neck and he was feeling her back, "We cannot do anything else. One day we will be through with this trial and be free of guards."

She agreed and she said, "That is nice! Does it feel nice with you?"

"It feels natural," he said.

He was dying, it felt so good. Be calm this is the first time she has let you kiss her and only one time. He told himself.

She said, "Kiss me and I am going to go bed."

They were panting and she grabbed a towel, "I never knew this about myself. NEVER would I have let you do this before now. I am so happy that I did! Did I do okay?"

"You are great!" He just kept kissing her gently.

"Thank you I needed to hear that."

Tate told her, "Wait until we are MARRIED and we can be free to do anything we want to do ... all day and all night!"

"Only if you want to?" he said and she nodded.

"This is the normal way two people make love ... not sex. I do love you. You do know that. Don't you?" Tate asked.

"When I get a job, I want you for my wife. Will you marry me?" staring into her eyes.

"Yes ... if you can treat me like this, I can TRUST you forever! Tate that was so wonderful and I do, do love you!" and she went quietly to bed.

He just stood and prayed this didn't happen again. He would make sure it didn't. He would protect her. He did not want her to get pregnant until they were married.

She was thinking, he has no idea that they had removed her uterus because she was so damaged. This would come out in the trial. Then he would not want her because she could not have children. His children, she began to cry and cry... the female guard came in and she told her she had had a night-mare and needed one of her sleeping pills.

Tate was dying to hold her, but he knew he couldn't, and it was killing him to hear her cry.

He knew the guard would be watching more closely the remainder of the night.

He stayed in his bed listening until she fell asleep.

He lay awake thinking how could anyone hurt this beautiful girl ... that he loved.

No one would ever hurt her again. She was his to take care of. Then he slept.

The town was abuzz about the impending trial. The lawyers from far and wide had been summoned by the parents. The jocks were not worried. They continued to terrorize the girls at school.

Girls made daily complaints to the principal, but nothing was done to the football team because they had been winning games this football season.

The SBI had the results of Coraine's test and the DNA of four of the team members were identified. They had minor police offenses that had required a mug shot and fingerprints and DNA filed. The other three had never been in legal trouble. If the judge requests, they could have mouth swabs done and it could be compared to the remaining three DNA found in the poor dead girl.

Reading the evidence Adriana had cringed. I have to win this one. I am going to call daddy and have him send me the best criminal lawyer he has to fight this school. She could see it was going to take an army. She had the SBI, Trevor, Roscoe, Guy, and now Unitus.

She had met with Debbie and interviewed her and got all her medical records and she saw that report. This was now haunting her. A sixteen year old's uterus had to be removed. The animals ... these boys were MURDERERS of all the unborn children, this girl could have had. This was going to be in my closing statement for sure.

Coraine, Tate's cousin, had given Adriana the most eye witness evidence. Coraine named the SEVEN and the team attacking Tate to get to Debbie was evidence. Thank goodness Roscoe took pictures of that boy's bruises.

When Adriana got home her husband was standing by the stove cooking! He had her apron on. He looked so cute. He had three recipe books laid out that he had got from Jana.

Really Jana had cooked it all. He was just going to pretend for today! He chuckled, "She is going to see right through this, Dude!" he said to himself.

He would learn but he'd need more lessons, and Bruce had kept talking while Jana was trying to teach him. He would have to remember to gag Bruce in the future, and he laughed.

Adriana dropped her briefcase, and kicked her heels off, and ran to plant a kiss on him. He said, "You know I'll burn dinner?" He took the pots off the stove.

"Oh what the heck! We can have dessert first!" he grinned.

They never had that week's honeymoon ... but now they were on there second week of bliss, and had not lighten the intensity.

"You are a superwoman! And I love it! I knew the first day I saw you on those courthouse steps that you were the one. Now I cannot live without you Adriana!"

"You never will. We will grow old together on this mountaintop. I do love it here! I'm hungry what have we for dinner ... my love?"

"Let me go look at the recipe book!" with a sheepish look on his face.

"Unitus you cooked and don't know what you cooked?"

He shook his head, "Haven't a clue! Guilty as charged."

"And who of the female persuasion has been in my kitchen?" glaring into his eyes.

"It was Bruce!" he looked at the ceiling.

"And who else?" not cracking a smile.

"And Jana. I cannot lie to my beautiful angel. They will be so disappointed in me ... They've known me to lie for many years," Unitus confessed.

"It was a good try and it is delicious. I was so afraid. If you didn't know what you put in it, I might end up in the emergency room! I can't get sick the trial is in two days." She took a mouthful of the tasty chicken whatever, and moaned. "This is sooo good! She will have to teach you again and you watch the next time."

"ONLY if you moan like that again will I consider it," and he gathered her up and stood her against the wall.

"Mercy! I didn't know you like me to moan? Ooh. Yum!"

She said as he raised her high and kissed her bellybutton.

She moaned and licked her lips. "Let's go have the main course on the couch. I don't think we will make it to the bedroom. She wrapped her legs around his waist. Unitus was so strong and she was so light that he had no problem getting her to the couch. He had no problem being man enough to let her do what she liked to do which was to undress him and by then he was moaning.

Afterward he said, "I love being MARRIED to you, angel. How about you?"

"I would never have thought. I'd love love love marriage!"

Beatrice and the twins were strolling over to Kyleigh when she saw some boys in the woods. Dynamite was barking and she patted his head. The guards saw them and chased them away. She bent down and kiss her doggie. The twins were unaware. They had gotten use to the dog's barking and they were best buds.

She told Roscoe about it. He spoke with the guards and they said they got pictures. "Holy Crap! It is two of the boys on trial." He faxed them to Trevor and Guy, so they could be aware and keep their dogs with them at all times.

Kyleigh said Black Velvet is with us Guy all the time I am not worried. He could see it in her eyes, she was anxious. She promised she would not take Madison out strolling without him.

The courtroom was filled to capacity. The big time lawyers had bought their press contacts so their performance could be documented for future hiring prospects. It was the IN thing to do in the judicial system. It drums up business, Adriana told Unitus. Her daddy had sent the best. His name was Alexander Graham Bell. What a name! Talking about attention, he was surely getting his share.

The parents were lined up behind the football team which were all dressed in suits and neckties. They had been charged and all were out on bail. None looked at Debbie and Tate with out displaying a mean fiendish look. Like SEVEN gargoyles sitting on a Gothic building, only they were sitting in court.

Madeline sat with Trevor, Beatrice sat with Roscoe, Jana sat with Bruce and Unitus. Unitus was so proud of his wife, he had watched her pouring over briefs until wee hours of the morning. The trial lawyer that sat beside her was presenting himself as sincere.

He could see that Debbie's teeth were chattering. Tate was not phased. The kid knew he had to be strong for her. That would calm her and he held her hand. She immediately relaxed. He stared at the goons. They knew, he could put them under. Their eyes said they were going to get him. Roscoe saw it too, as did Trevor. Trevor never got riled about anything but this was making his temperature rise.

Especially their smirking and laughter before the judge came in, and the court was bought to order and they all rose.

The honorable Judge Bernice Porter presiding, "You may be seated."

The charges were read and the opening arguments were presented. Adriana was dramatic. Unitus was mesmerized.

He had never seen her in action and this was an important case. Little did he know that she had put away a mafia ring and a serial killer. She was not one to brag, and he was finding out that he may have to hire a few guards for her. That he was going to be discussing with Roscoe, before this day was done.

He hated to be dependent on anyone for security, but his legs could not chase anyone through the woods. He had the judo skills and a black belt degree for anyone that came close.

He was a superb marksman, but needed to get his weaponry from his apartment. That would be done. He had been in an intense weight program while recuperating and was strong enough to take down the best.

He was going to expand to blade training. He had a leg with a blade that he had not used yet. This was his new goal running at top speed ... All these things were running through his mind as the court adjoined for lunch.

He shook Alexander's hand while he lunched with his wife.

He asked if he was married and he was. His wife, Candice was a ballet instructor and they had three lovely daughters.

Bell opened his wallet and showed his girls off. Adriana was oohing and awwing. "They are so cute." She looked at

Unitus and said, "I want one!" and he blew her a kiss. That was going to be his next goal, not blade running and he was grinning. She saw that out of the corner of her eye and took her shoe off and rubbed it on his good shin.

He had beads of sweat popping out on his forehead. He said, "Waiter oh waiter can I get a glass of nothing, but ICE. He was looking straight at Adriana and his eyes were saying "wait until I get you home." Her eyes were saying, "I can't wait either."

The first week the evidence was being presented and the parents were looking at their boys as if to say "you were raised better than this." One of the mother's was crying. Their lawyers were not prepared and it was obvious these boys should be behind bars, if not for due process "innocent until proven guilty", they would be.

Unitus had seen a lot in his few years on this earth but this, turned his stomach. When his wife recited what these little punks had done to that little girl. The report of the damage was so bad, they took out her uterus. Debbie fainted.

Tate was holding her. He did not care who saw him. He had tears coming down the side of his face. The medic was there with ammonia to bring Debbie around. She opened her eyes and said to Tate, "Now you know. I'm not normal." She sat stone-faced.

Trevor was clenching his teeth and Madeline was trying to calm him. She was so glad Kyleigh had not come and Guy was staying with her.

The nurses, Angie and Laurie were caring for the boys one at each house, plus the dogs were at the the houses.

The courtroom had gone berserk and the gavel was beating "Order in the court! Order in the court!"

There was to be no cameras in the courtroom, but reporters were recording. After adjournment, outside the flashbulbs began nonstop ... They were chasing people for interviews and news media were in the rampant crowds filming. It was a circus!

Adriana was not phased because she and Alexander were use to it. It was just another day at the office for them. Trevor told the SBI they needed to move the kids to his house and bring their agents there. "We have twenty bedrooms SO do it!"

They brought the cars around back and screened the teens and put them in the white limo and the black cars were in front and the black cars were in the back, a massive escort.

Debbie had laid her head on Tate's shoulder. Trevor told him, "TATE you are one of us now. So it is time you came home."

Madeline nodded, "Debbie I am here for you," and she patted her leg.

Roscoe was gathering his men and making assignments to cover Adriana and Unitus. This was worse than he could have ever imagined.

Trevor had never dreamed his service buddies would have to help protect his family. Roscoe's men were too few in number for this.

The most trustworthy maids and caterers were called to care for Trevor's family. He didn't even want them going to the grocery store by themselves. Who knew who was related to these seven boys' parents ... kin, coaches, and lawyers out there in the community that could do collateral damage.

This trial was going to tear this little town apart. Trevor was going to try and hold it together, if it killed him.

As they gathered around the long dining room table, Tate and Debbie felt LOVE, like they had never had before. This family truly loved them. Trevor said grace and they bowed and gave thanks.

Bruce and Jana helped situate the SBI in their rooms and Trevor felt good about them using his well equipped office.

The other horses has arrived today and they were adjusting well. The electric fence was set for any two legged or four legged creatures. The guards were on their posts. His home was secure.

Everyone said good night and Tate walked Debbie to her assigned room. One of the female officer would be sharing her room. One of the male officers would be sharing with Tate. All the rooms on the top floor had double beds.

Debbie hugged him and said, "I feel safer here and it is so beautiful. It started out a horrible day … but it has ended in a happy place."

Tate said, "Yes, is has! Trevor adopting me has changed my life. I owe it all to Roscoe. Sleep well and nothing that was said in the court makes any difference in the way I feel about you. Goodnight, my happy girl," and he kissed her quickly on the lips. She looked sad.

He added, "I know better than kissing you the way that I want to …" and she smiled and closed her eyes.

"I'll dream of that! Goodnight," and walked into her room.

CHAPTER SEVEN

Beatrice asked Roscoe about what she can do for Tate and Debbie? He said kissing her, "Pray. See you tonight. Keep that dog by your side. Love you! " He kissed Cain and Caleb and he was out the door like a whirlwind.

Roscoe was trying to cover all the bases, but those BOYS in the woods had unnerved him. They were too close to his home and up to no good. After facing them in the courtroom and hearing the depth of evil that they possessed, he would not put anything pass them. They were capable of harming his family. These boys had no consciences.

He was getting angrier by the minute and that was not good.

He went by Trevor's and Madeline, and said I need to talk.

He shared his anger with Trevor and they agreed to be each others sounding boards.

Trevor said, "Madeline is already worried about my anger. So I have to do a better job of hiding it. You my boy are amazing, you must have ESP? You knew I needed to talk!"

In walks Guy, "Yes he does! He has ESP and a gift of gab!"

Roscoe pretended sparring with Guy, "The gab ... I got from you, Bro!"

Tate walked in, "I must be dreaming. This family likes to fight!" he laughed with them.

"Roscoe and I have been sparring for years! We just might invest in some boxing gloves one day," Guy said.

"That's a great idea. I read ... it can relieve tension," Trevor said.

Guy and Roscoe continued to pretend sparring and included Tate in their air punches. Tate smiled.

Roscoe said, "I have a wife and twins that drain my tension ..." still sparring and dodging Tate's and Guy's jabs.

"Me too, Bro but this is the worse I have anger about what was done to Kyleigh." He punched the air so hard, "and now what has been done to Debbie." Almost missing the wall, where Roscoe backed him.

"Bro, you got to talk to me ... us?" Roscoe shook Guy.

"She started screaming last night ... flashbacks ... the dog went wild. I have another door to replace ... Kyleigh is my world. This trial is something I can't hide from her ...What am I going to do?" Guy was holding his head and bending over.

Trevor had Tate to the side, "Let's go get some breakfast."

On the way he explained about what happened to Kyleigh.

Tate said, "Thanks Trevor. I didn't know Roscoe nor Guy when it was going on ... I am so sorry. Sounds like Debbie may have some of the same in the future. I also have to come clean ..."

Trevor looked at him, "Go on ... talk to me like Roscoe is talking to Guy."

"I have asked Debbie to marry me in the future," he was out of breath, but he got it out.

"Is that all?" Trevor looked at him. Tate nodded.

"For a minute I thought you were going to tell me something bad. That is great news!" they both smiled.

"I know I promised to go to college but I don't know … if I can wait that long." Tate was looking at the floor scared of what Trevor was going to say next.

"Who said you have to wait? You can do both," patting Tate on the shoulder and laughing out loud.

Madeline came around the corner, "Did I miss something? I need a good laugh, too" Trevor kissed her.

Tate was smiling and they both hugged him.

Trevor said, "Seems you have to teach the boy something and something quick!"

Tate's mouth flew open and Madeline's mouth flew open, both in shock.

"Both you two shut your mouths … This is a secret!!!" motioning for him to get in a huddle with he and Madeline.

"Madeline you have to teach Tate to shop online. Tate she loves to shop!" Madeline punched Trevor's on the shoulder and Tate was grinning.

Madeline asked Tate what he needed and they would shop.

"An engagement ring for Debbie … I have already ask her to marry me way before yesterday … she just needs to know I still want her … especially with this trial!" Tate said with pleading eyes.

"Tate there is one thing you need to know about women," Madeline said as Debbie walked into the kitchen.

She looked so sad.

Tate said, "What Miss Madeline?" gulping.

Debbie was confused. Tate was looking at her crazily and Madeline was looking at her and she was about to cry.

Madeline said, "Tate told me you might like to pick your own engagement ring out. Would you? We can go online and have it on your finger by noon!"

Debbie was smiling so bright the sun was the only thing to compare it to and Tate kissed her in front of everyone. She sat down quickly because her legs were weak, and both Trevor and Madeline smiled at the young couple.

"Now who wants breakfast?" Roscoe and Guy had come in and heard the news and were slapping Tate on the back. "Congrats, Bro. Congrats!"

Tate was smiling, matching Debbie's smile. Not only was he engaged to the love of his life but … he was now a BRO!

All four men said, "I do. I'm starving."

"Didn't your wives feed you?" Madeline asked.

"Yes ma'am but you cook better!" Roscoe and Guy said it at the same time.

Trevor told Debbie, "They say that every time. She needs to teach you her cooking skills."

Madeline said, "Sure I will as soon as I teach you to shop online!"

In unison Roscoe and Guy both looked at Tate and said, "Welcome to our world, Bro!"

Tate turned his head to the side as if he hadn't a clue what they were talking about, and looked at Trevor to explain.

"You will learn. You will learn. Got a feeling the wives will be teaching Debbie how to control you like they do us!"

They all laughed.

Madeline winked at Debbie. After eating they got on the computer and found what Debbie liked and ordered.

Then they got in the cars with their escorts and went to the courthouse.

Tate and Debbie didn't let anything that was said that day affect them. All they could do was sit and hold hands. Squeezing them occasionally and looking back at Trevor and Madeline who were smiling at them.

At lunch the ring was delivered and Tate got down on one knee in the restaurant and officially proposed. The restaurant patrons cheered.

Guy had not gone to the courthouse today but stayed with Kyleigh. She and he played with Madison.

He asked her, if she would like to go for a picnic. He was trying to occupy her mind with good stuff. "Bring your camera. You can take some of Madison in your favorite places."

They did make it a fun day and were so tired when they got back home, they all fell asleep without watching TV.

During the night, Guy checked the computer for the daily news to see what had happened. He was glad nothing new would be broadcast, then he could sleep the night. Madison had been sleeping all night since last month.

When he got in bed, Kyleigh said, "I wanted to properly thank my husband for this day!" He was moaning.

Debbie and Tate could hardly wait to get home from court. She was showing her ring to everyone at supper. Tate could not keep his hands off her. Trevor told the female officer to give them some privacy tonight. Trevor was smart enough to know if they didn't get alone time, they may go in the woods and those boys not going to get their hands on his kids. He must talk to Tate now.

"Tate I know how confining it can be in this house. Especially when you are in love, but you will have alone time. I have spoken to the female guard. You and Debbie can not walk in the woods, do you hear me! I was once young believe it or not, and have taken many a girl to lover's lane in the woods. These woods are not safe ... Two of the boys on trial were spotted out back of Roscoe's house. He sent me the pictures. So they maybe in our woods. The SBI and Roscoe's men are on alert for them. I can't have you two in danger."

Tate was mortified and shook his head.

Trevor said, "I need to know whether you want one or two hours of free time?"

Tate's face turned red, "One hour will be good. Thank you! You are teaching me every day how to take care of my wife! Of myself too! I need to check on my aunt and the cousins. I hate to ask. You have done so much for me."

"I understand call her but if we go by ... they may target them. I will have a couple of men guard the house since the boys are so unstable. Glad you brought that to my attention. I don't want anyone hurt by them I will be so glad when they are behind bars for a long ... long time."

"Thank you, sir for everything," they hugged and he went to see Debbie. She was sitting on the sofa in her bedroom.

"I love you so much," she said and fell into his arms.

"I never knew what true love was until I met you. I will make you a good husband. Trevor said we did not have to wait till I finished college to get married. So think about when you want to?" Tate gazed into her eyes.

"Tomorrow would be good," she said.

"How about tonight?" he was kissing her so that she was writhing and he was grinding into her.

He jerked back, "Did I hurt you?"

"No but I think I need a shower," she said.

"OH God Do I need a shower," he said.

They undressed and took a long shower ... Nothing more.

"I got one hour and I have to be dressed and out of here. Don't do that pleaseeee!" Tate said.

"Yes, I want you with me tonight and every night. Ask Madeline tomorrow... if we can get married online and that will solve everything."

"I have to go. Talk to Madeline! Goodnight, my happy girl! I love you." Then he kissed her and she said, "I Love You!"

It took two days to order the dress and tuxedo, and get the license. They indeed could get married online by Skype.

Trevor ask them, "Why would you go online for a minister when I can marry you in the living room or by the pool or wherever you two want?" Their eyes lit up.

All the family came that Sunday and they were MARRIED by the swimming pool. It was a sweet ceremony. Cake and ice cream was served afterward.

The female guard named Enya whispered to Tate, "Guess I got to clear out?"

Tate said, "Yes, ma'am. You can have my room," and his male guard named Clarence smiled.

Clarence said, "Sounds good to me!"

Enya stated firmly, "I have a roommate and she is prettier than you!"

Enya whispered to Debbie, "And I ain't talking about you honey, but I needed to put him in his place. That will keep him from coming around me." Winking at Madeline which knew, she was not gay and she had herself a good laugh.

Tate moved into Debbie's room and they put a sign on the bedroom door that said, "JUST MARRIED."

PART TEN

CHAPTER ONE

Aunt Eunice was so glad to hear from Tate. She was still mourning Coraine's death. She could not believe what the news was saying about her daughter. Blaming herself for not knowing about the rape or the drugs.

She had to ask Tate. "Did you know?"

"Yes ... she told me she was going with me to the drug rehab center? She begged me not to tell you!" he said.

"There was nothing you nor I could have done. I am just so sad. Jennifer came for a little while. Let me give you her number at college. I know you can't come over here. I have seen the court case on TV. Corey is in a skateboard contest. He would love to talk to you. Jason says Hi ... I'm talking away ... How are you?" she asked.

"You talk all you need to... I wish I could come over ... maybe soon. Trevor has adopted me my last name is Porter now. I and Debbie are married. I ask Trevor to protect you all from those boys on trial, so if you see two guards or men walking and looking around your house, don't be frightened. If you need anything this is his number. I am not allowed to go out till the trial ends nor is Debbie. She sends her love."

"We love you Tate!" his aunt meant it. He told her the same.

Adriana and Unitus had been working on their baby plans all weekend, now on Monday she was stepping high.

Alexander Bell said "You must have on a new pair of shoes or could it be Unitus?"

She said, "You are so observant counselor. Is your smile because you went home to see Candice and had a good weekend?"

He replied, "You are so observant counselor and yes she always puts a smile on my face."

They were still walking into the court room and stopped to take their places and arrange their papers.

Adriana turned to see her clients and they flashed her their rings, and she smiled.

She was going to work even harder for these two.

The days dragged by with one testimony after another of the results of the findings.

Adriana requested that 3 of the boys have hair follicle or mouth swabs done within the courtroom, so there would be no mix up on the outside. This was done and the young men were not happy nor were their lawyers.

With the results returning, all seven members of the football team were placed under arrest when the DNA was read to the judge that every single one was found in the vagina of the dead girl. The medical examiner's report revealed that it was humanly impossible for this victim to have been able to inject herself from three of the sites that drugs had been infused. The Judge stated there would be no bond set for any of them.

The jury's verdict was read three weeks later. Guilty on all counts. Each received life sentences for MURDER and added 15 years to each for rape.

This was spread all over the TV news, newspaper, radio and discussed on almost every talk show day and night.

The school was in fear of being sued, but victory was sweet as far as this family was concerned. Someone else could sue the school.

The school had fired the coach and new guidelines were in place about sexual harassment and sexual abuse.

Alexander asked Adriana, "Are you sure? This is the time to go for the jugular," in reference to the school.

Adriana responded, "Not this time. If they make a misstep, they know I will be after them. I live in this town. I appreciate your help. Tell father, strike that ...I will tell him. Tell Candice to be good to you. She will know what I mean. KISS KISS."

He was on the plane and Unitus was standing beside her.

"I like that KISS KISS and no TOUCH TOUCH, I came for both. I am taking you somewhere romantic for a real honey-moon. Where do you want to go?" he asked.

"On top of a mountain where the sunset is visible from a black leather couch and I can see it rise the next morning and set and rise and set."

Unitus cringed and pulled her to him, "You just have to do that to me in public. Don't you?"

"You betcha! I must keep practicing till we cannot breath another breath," she licks her lips.

He picked her up, "Did you make the Doctor's appointment? Stop or I will drop you?"

"I made it and we can go tomorrow together and get the results," kissing him thoroughly while standing by the airport fence.

He said, "Why would you do that here?"

She said, "I have crotchless undies and a short skirt. Why wouldn't I?"

"You love to live on the edge. Don't you?" he gasped.

"Don't you? See that tree and those bushes. I will let you walk real close to me till we get there. Then you are on your own," she instructed.

"NO … I call the shots for a change!" Unitus stated.

He took his coat off which was huge, three times wider than she, and put it around her back, and tucked it into his pockets.

"Now that's solved … do your job prosecutor," he smiled.

He was still hold her looking into her eyes as she unbuckled and fit her crotchless panties over him and her mouth flew open and he sealed it with his … slowly ever so slowly. No one could see a thing just two people kissing!

"Was it good for you?" she took her legs down that she had wrapped around his waist and stood talking not touching.

"Are you through, I'm not," He frowned. She came for him.

He said, "I was just kidding!" She hit his stomach with her purse.

"Don't you will knock me off my leg cause then I will hurt myself," he was laughing so hard.

"You will be charged with spousal abuse." He was rubbing it in.

"I will abuse you when I get you home," she said.

"Promise? Can I drive this time?" she had turned her back to him.

When she turned, he was holding two tickets to Paris for one week. Reservation confirmed at the Hotel de Vendome Paris1. She was reading and her mouth was not saying anything. She was either in shock or happy.

"I know my wife is a lawyer and she is fluent at legal jargon but at this moment could she speak a little louder to her husband about whether or not she likes the idea or does not? or if SHE wants to make other arrangements? Please answer one or all of the above, Adriana?"

Her mouth was moving, but there was no sound.

"KISS" she pointed to her lips.

"I can't ... we may be arrested. Can't take the chance!"

He took her by the hand and instructed her to get in the van that HE was driving. She still couldn't form words.

He said, "I know it has been a tough week or three weeks actually, and I know we have been going at it for this child we both want."

He looked and she was sound asleep. "Man, it is quiet ... I must have done a bang up job. She sleeps like that every time afterward ... but more so lately ... Hmm." He smiled all the way home.

They went to the OB-GYN and it was confirmed she was pregnant.

She said, "You have given me everything I have wanted."

He said, "You have given me everything I have wanted."

The Doctor said, "Would you two like me to leave?"

They said in unison, "You betcha!"

You can have this room for thirty minutes and that is all.

They never stopped staring at each other.

In unison, "Thanks Doc!"

The Doctor wrote a note and taped it to the door,

> ROOM OCCUPIED...
> DO NOT ENTER PER
> DR.SILVERSTEIN.

"I mean all you Nurses!"

The doctor left a note at the check-out desk, "This was your baby shower gift, Adriana & Unitus. Signed, Silverstein

Adriana said, "That is a cheap present?"

Unitus said, "I kinda liked it!" He swatted her buttocks.

Adriana said, "Legally my insurance paid for that and I can have him arrest for insurance fraud."

Unitus said, "You wouldn't dare?" A terrified look on his face.

Adriana cackled, "Do you think I am crazy?"

Unitus admitted, "Sometimes!"

She swatted him, "I would do nothing to this precious doctor. He is going to deliver our baby, darling!"

She grinned at him and he said, "Do not kiss me in public!"

Tate and Debbie went straight to Aunt Eunice's house. She hugged and hugged them.

Corey was 15 years old now. His blond hair was darkening under his favorite Yankee's baseball cap. His freckles barely visible. His hazel eyes bore into you as he talked about skateboarding. Tate listened and nodded occasionally. That he had learned from Roscoe. When he wanted to talk, Roscoe would nod for him to go on. Corey was excited to show him his long board for racing and his short board for tricks. Tate got him talking about his tricks.

"Just wheelies and kick flips. Not any parks around that I can get to. Same as when you were here."

They had walked a couple of blocks and turned around heading back home, "so mostly I go to the school parking lot.

People come down on me, if I get on the sidewalk. Just something to do!"

He was kicking rocks on the road as they walked, "I make ramps and jump bars that kind of stuff. Not much else to do around here. I hope one day to get into it full time. Just got to get the better equipment. They say if you are good enough, companies will pay you to advertize for them. Wouldn't that be awesome? A kid like me from a small town. Don't stand a chance. You and Debbie coming over will make mom happy."

Corey nodded at Tate, "Yeah ... It will. Thanks man. Good to have you back!"

Tate had to ask before they got back to the house, "How's Aunt Eunice doing?"

"She's not crying as much ... at least, if she is ... I don't hear her. It was real bad at first." They were walking and talking as they got to the porch.

"Glad you finally came and seen us," he had to say it again.

"We knew you couldn't. I have not had anyone to talk to ... Been rough," Corey pulled at his baseball cap and turned it backwards. "You can come over now that the trial's over more often, can't you?"

"You bet. How's school going?" stopping to lean up against the house, not wanting to go in yet.

"Not good. Can't concentrate at home. Probably going to fail," shrugging his shoulders. "Hope not! That would hurt, mom. She says dad wanted all of us to graduate. I think that's why Jennifer did all that … to get into college. I miss her. She would let me talk like you do, Tate." He patted Corey on the back.

"What do you need to get you back on track? Books? Computer? Want me to help you?" Tate asked.

"That would be great!" they fist bumped him and they made plans to meet at the library twice weekly. Tate told him he studied twice weekly at the library with his friend Roscoe.

"Awesome. Guess we better go in, Jason's giving Mom a fit by now. She can't move, if I'm not around to horseplay with him. I can actually help him with HIS homework! The kid is just eleven, but he thinks he is a grownup. Bosses me around and I let him. Mom don't spank him like she did me. He gets by with a lot!" They laughed. He put the skateboard on a wall hook. They went on in the house. They could hear the females chattering. Corey high- fived Tate.

Aunt Eunice was talking to Debbie like she use to. The way that she never could with Coraine.

They stopped talking when they heard them coming in the back door. Tate was glad his aunt could talk to Debbie. She needed girl talk and she was admiring Debbie's rings.

"So you two, really did get married!" She looked at Tate's wedding band. "I'm so proud of you two. The Porters must be wonderful people."

Debbie said, "Yes they are. We would be dead … if they weren't!" She covered her mouth. "I am so sorry. I don't know why I said that!"

"It's the truth! Don't feel bad. I love you guys! Nothing makes me happier than to know you are safe," Aunt Eunice hugged each one again.

"The meanies are put away that hurt my Coraine. If it wasn't for you, they would be out there hurting other people tonight. You did good Tate. You are the reason Debbie will be a good wife, Tate. I expect to see more of you both!"

"When Jennifer comes home for a visit call me. I want to see her and Tate does, too," Debbie said.

"If Jennifer hadn't helped me, I would have not been able to get my scholarship. I am looking forward to going to college," Tate admitted.

His cousin Jennifer was the reason he went to the library. If he had not gone, he would never have met Roscoe.

Corey said, "That is awesome! Maybe I can hit the books more!"

Aunt Eunice's eyes popped wide, "Unbelievable! I have been trying to get him to do that all year. You waltz in and … I am thankful!"

Corey told her about going to the library after school two days a week. She was almost in tears.

"Aww don't do that again," Corey said and hugged her.

"These are happy tears son, leave me be!" she wiped at her eyes with her apron.

They had brought them supper and they sat as a family and ate. Even Jason was sitting still, and his mom was patting him on the back.

They left when Roscoe came by and drove them home.

"How was your visit?" They were smiling and Tate said it was long over due.

"I owe her a lot for taking me in. I need to go to the library twice a week to help Corey with his homework … until he gets the hang of studying like you helped me."

"That will be my honor to help him, too. I feel there are still a lot of angry people in this town right now, so I don't want neither of you going out until it settles down. We will check on some wheels for you to drive then. Okay, that sound good Mr and Mrs Tate Porter?"

"Don't don't don't hug me when I am driving! How would it look, if I had a wreck!" Roscoe looked both ways and down the long road to Southfork. They were enjoying the ride home.

CHAPTER TWO

Madeline had finally made her appointment at DUKE. She felt her breast cancer had come back and her oncologist scheduled her for a mammogram. She was not going to worry Trevor and she said, "Honey I have to go for my routine checkup May 23rd at 11:00AM. Can you go with me?"

"What kind of question is that? You know I will," Trevor was eying her closely.

"Are you feeling okay, honey? I know I have been busy, but you are my first priority and you know it," he stated.

GM smiled at him, "It is a month away so we can plan a day and night away from the children. Really we need it?"

"I think a weekend retreat would be good to tack onto that Friday!" putting his arm around her. They watched the sunset.

In comes the newlyweds, "We're home!" kissing Trevor and Madeline on the cheek.

"How was you 'all visit and supper?" Madeline asked.

"It made my Aunt Eunice and my cousins very happy," Tate said smiling.

Debbie said, "They wanted me to thank you for all you two have done for my husband and me." She looked at Tate who had not heard her call him her husband. His chest was expanding because he was so proud.

"She had a fit over my diamond!" She held it up to the light like she herself could not believe it was real.

"She looks at it every hour. I woke up in the middle of the night and she had her hand up to the light looking at it ... about blinded me! In the middle of the night ... Trevor," Tate said shaking his head.

Debbie elbowed him.

"It's a woman thing, Son. They do that so you will give them more jewelry," Madeline elbowed Trevor.

"Ohhh Okay!" Tate rubbed his forehead. "I sure have got a lot to learn. Best we say goodnight. See ya in the morning."

Debbie and he walked to their room. She was giggling.

Trevor turned to Madeline, "Do you want any more jewelry? I am not good at remembering birthdays."

He reached in his coat pocket and pulled out a box, "Happy Birthday darling!" kissing her hand. "I didn't forget!"

She opened the rectangular box and inside there was a diamond and sapphire bracelet and he fastened it onto her wrist. He was so thoughtful.

"I forgot myself. I am really happy one of us remembered. Let's go next month and celebrate."

"Are you saying you have your first headache?"

"Yep got a doozie!" he saw she was not joking and helped her to their room.

"Why didn't you say something before now?" Trevor was concerned.

"I just thought it would go away and I enjoy my husband's company."

He helped her into bed, she took two tablets, and she slept.

"Roscoe, big guy! How are the newlyweds doing?" she asked as he came into the nursery. Cain was standing holding onto his mother's leg. Caleb was sitting and pulling animals from the toy bin.

When they saw their daddy, Cain got so excited he took two steps and sat squealing with his arms raised for his daddy to pick him up.

Caleb got so excited he pulled the entire bin into the floor and looked at Roscoe, then back to the bin with his little mouth wide open. It looked like he was deciding which would be more fun. Then he started waddling as fast as he could toward Roscoe.

Roscoe had them both up in the air playing airplane while his beautiful wife sat holding her back. She had no vomiting with this pregnancy, but back pain at four months was probably from toting the twins.

"How is my little darling doing?" by then he had each boy under each of his arms, and was bending to kiss Beatrice's red hair and stare into her pale green eyes.

She roared like a lion.

He said, "That's a good sign. Leo the lion needs to be tamed. I'll see what I can do about that tonight."

"But first my hero you need nourishment. I have a roast in the oven and potato salad in the fridge. I'm just going to sit here for a bit. Those steps are killing my back. Can I live downstairs OR ....?" she laughed and laughed.

"Okay, honey share … boys, boys your mother is fixing to speak, so listen" so he sat at her feet having to prop the boys up so all three of them were looking up at her. "This is going to be funny cause she is laughing."

"Roscoe dear husband … " placing her hand on his cheek.

"UH OH … this is the I want laugh. What might my darling wife want?"

The boys looked like little monkeys hanging from a tall tree as Roscoe stood.

"I want to have a chairlift like a little old woman put on the staircase," and she burst out crying. His hands were full with the boys and all he could do was say.

"Okay … done! My little twin making mama … can have anything her heart desires," he was talking to the boys.

"Anything!" he had his eyebrows going up and down.

"I'll take the boys down and we'll eat while you take a nap. If you want and I'll bring you some … food … dessert back up and feed it to my little old woman."

She threw a pillow at him and said, "You are so sweet." She blew him a kiss while lying down on the sofa in the boys room.

The boys were fed and were so worn out from playing with their daddy that they were fast asleep when he kissed her awake.

She smiled and said, "I was just dreaming about you, Fabio. What might you be after. I bet a massage. Come closer and let me rub your back. My man has been working so HARD... that his muscles are all tense." She rubbed ALL his tension away.

Kyleigh and Guy took Madison and Black Velvet down to Madeline and Trevor's. The stroller was Madison's favorite toy. If he wasn't in it, he was pushing it.

Madison was going to be a race car driver for sure. Kyleigh had got her figure back and had on a summer dress that was transparent as she walked in the sun. She kept getting sexier and sexier. She had asked if she could wear her skinny jeans.

"You know better," and he smiled at her holding tight to her hand and giving it a squeeze.

She had a twinkle in her eyes, this walk was invigorating. How on earth was he going to give this up. Daily adventures with his wife. He was going to ask GM, if he could reopen GM & GS Private Investigation Service.

He had too much free time and people had expressed a need for his expertise. So he had talked to Kyleigh. She said, "Whatever makes you happy, I'm for it. You can't BABYSIT me forever."

"I am not doing that. I don't want to miss a step of Madison life. I guess because my dad wasn't around and granddad was always working. Now I can be the Dad ... I always wanted. Do you understand?" Guy asked Kyleigh.

Looking into his eyes, "I've always known it." Her smile was bright as the sunshine. Her sundress was flapping in the wind exposing her beautiful legs. "You just needed to say it out loud for yourself. You are a wonderful father," kissing him. She knew better than kissing him on the mouth.

Madison was pushing the stroller and the dog was walking step for step with him.

Guy loved the way his family had moved near to them. Kyleigh was more secure and open about how she felt. The trial had ended so the drama had ended. It was a peaceful atmosphere now at their home. No more nightmares and flashbacks for two months.

They had finally reached the house around the bend. Blackie & Magic met their offspring Black Velvet and it was a sweet reunion. They frolicked in the yard and the barking brought Madeline and Trevor out on the veranda.

They worried about Madison around the swimming pool and promised to have an instructor to come and teach him to swim from an early age. Til then they would watch him close.

Hugs and kisses. Guy had Madeline something in his pocket and he pulled it out and handed it to her. "Happy Birthday GM. You thought I forgot? Never!"

"Well SHE forgot until I reminded her," Trevor stated.

She opened the box and there was a diamond and sapphire pin shaped like her dog. She smiled and a tear dropped. "How did you get this made with all the chaos of the trial?"

"Where there's a will, there's a way," kissing her on the cheek.

The newlyweds came out and had no idea it was Madeline's birthday and apologized for no gift.

"Don't worry! I have tired to forgot how old I am getting." They all went to the restaurant THE INN and had birthday cake. It was what GM needed to cheer her up.

Debbie told Tate she was going to make a booklet of all the families' birthdays and he agreed that was a good idea.

Roscoe, Beatrice, and the twins had brought Madeline a gift and as they ate cake, she opened the little box. It was a sapphire locket with their picture in it.

Tate said, "Trevor you told me women liked jewelry. I think everyone knows Miss Madeline likes sapphires, but me!"

Trevor said, "She likes diamonds more!" They all laughed as he patted his wallet.

She said, "I love my family more than all the diamonds and sapphires in the world."

All raised a toast and said," Here! Here!" That was their family's special cheer.

CHAPTER THREE

Adriana spoke to the DA office and cleared her calendar for the dates of their honeymoon trip. Unitus had really surprised her. She had not an inkling that he was planning this wonderful getaway.

With the news that Unitus was going to be a father, it had him pumping iron everyday. He wanted to be in top physical shape for his honeymoon. He knew his wife was doing the same in her Pilates class.

They were loving the idea of shopping together for the baby. It was a good thing Roscoe's bachelor pad had a spare bedroom. She was already having a design team to look at it and present some different ideas for the nursery courtesy of her father.

They had Skype him and told him, he was going to be a grandfather and how much they appreciated Alexander Bell helping with the court case.

"When we get back … Daddy you have to come and see our mountain retreat. It is spectacular to see the sunset from our glass living room," Adriana told him.

"Glass living room?" Marcus asked.

"The window is from one wall to the other and it is like being an eagle sitting in a nest on the side of this huge mountaintop. Unitus thinks he is king of the mountain," Adriana detailed everything. Swatting him with the dish towel as he let out a Tarzan yell into the phone.

"I am and don't you forget it pretty Lady Long Legs," Unitus teased.

"OH No you didn't! Daddy I got to go. Talk later!" and she ran and jumped on him. He caught her.

"You cannot do that anymore. You are pregnant! You might upset junior in there!" he kissed her abs.

"I guess you are right! Hmm … This means I can have no fun on our honeymoon because we might hurt the baby," she sat with her pouty lip.

If he ever took a picture of that pose, he could really make her gravel at his feet. Dallas courtroom and this uptown courtroom here would have a field day with that picture!

Of course, they would never see this side of Adriana. It was only reversed for him.

She was through pouting and all hell was fixing to break lose. "What are we having for dinner?" She kicked her high heels off, and began unbuttoned her blouse very very slowly.

"I don't I don't I don't know. What would you like?" He was way across the room. He was licking his lips.

"I got to get a shower and we can gooo out if you waaant!"

She was unzipping her skirt. It fell to the floor. She had no panties on and unhooked the bra with a flick. "I think I need a shower worse than you. I have long legs that need washing. I can't reach them when" she was up against the wall. "When when I'm doing my husband a favorrrr," she said slowly and licked her lips.

"What favor might that be?" he begged to know.

"Not jumping on him!" then she turned and walked off. He followed her into the bedroom.

"Now honey the baby does need to exercise. I was just joking, Sweetums." He tried to kiss her. She turned her head.

"That's Lady Long Legs to you and don't you forget it!"

He scooped her up and took her to the shower. She was giggling. "That's more like my macho man," and she begin undressing him. He left his leg on and tennis shoe so he would not fall. She thought he was going to sit in the chair and she was pleasantly surprised how he was needing her.

"Now what were you saying?" Unitus asked.

"That my husband has ….. the largest most capable … hands that handle this wife of his … in all the right places!"

She was a feather weight to him, he did not want to hurt her but she was begging so loudly. He put her long legs around his waist and leaned against the wall as her long skinny fingers wrapped and guided him in all the right positions she liked. Anything she liked, he liked better. They were made for each other. They knew it from DAY ONE.

They dressed and went out to a Chili's in the area and got a mile high hamburger for a mile high appetite.

He had a beer and she had a "Tall Tall glass of water, please!" Looking Unitus in the eyes.

"You scared that poor waiter to death, counselor!" he said before he chomped on his burger.

"It's going to get worse! Yep going to get worse!" she sneered.

"What are you talking about now my love?" with a puzzled look on his face.

"I can't have a beer, martini, screwdriver! Just to name a few … cause I am pregnant!" then she smiled.

"I am PG and so happy. You have made me so happy and I get to drive everywhere when my husband drinks … can't have him getting arrested over a beeeeer."

"I thank you for taking such good care of me, wifey!" he said leaning to get a kiss.

It was dark in the corner and she reached under the table and grabbed him. "I'll always take care of my little man."

"What do you want boy or girl?" she asked and stared at him while she was devouring a straw licking all ends of that straw.

"What was that you were saying, honey, Sweetums?" he asked. "Take that straw and throw it under the table! Please! I can't think when you are sucking on it!"

"Okay! So you don't know what you want a male or female child?" she said and sipped her water as if she was sipping tea.

"I want a cute little girl that looks like you and has my manners!" he was grinning. "NO strike that. I want her like you to terrorize her husband as you do me. It is what makes me love you. Please Please do that … again!" he was gritted his teeth because of what she was doing under the table.

"That creative little mind in there … It challenges me to capture every moment and stow it away for the next adventure. WOW we are NEVER going to be bored like some folks and I never am going to be able to get up out of this seat … if you don't stop!"

"Complain complain, that's all I hear!" She gave him a big smile and blew him a kiss. "I have to go. You want to come?"

"NO thanks, I'll sit this one out!" he was so in love with his wife. Everyone in the restaurant knew who she was because of the magnitude of this week's trial. She is so poised in the courtroom, and she makes him feel ten feet tall. If he had two legs, she would climb him as she did before the accident.

"I just can't believe how lucky I am, woman!" as she slid in beside him and patted his artificial leg.

"I can't believe how lucky I am that you gave me a second chance. What you say we go rub the baby and rock her all night long?" she said.

"Pig" he said.

"Hog, and don't you forget it! See how this city girl has fit right in!"

"You'd fit right in anywhere," kissing her.

"Get in buster. I remember a man with a cobalt blue double breasted Armani suit, the dude that sweep me off my heels."

"Shows you agents come in all different characters. That definitely wasn't me. I was just playing the part," he grinned.

"I love the you, you are now. That character terrified me. He was dressed like a man my daddy would like," she stated.

"You mean when he comes I have to be the clean shaven businessman again?" he pretended to fume getting in the van.

"He won't care what you look like as long as you make his daughter happy ... and I'm happy!" she smiled and spun off.

Bruce and Jana had been to see her parents. Jana's mother loved her Brucie. Her father was more reserved. Bruce was uneasy because Mao Jung was not a happy man. His wife did not have to know, how badly he wanted to catch that kingpin. He was going to lay low this trip.

If he could get him, it would be a great negotiating piece for his trial. His loyal men were still in this area. There had to be a way. His worse fear would be that they would harm Jana so he would not go there.

They had a good visit and the parents promised to come for a visit before the summer was over. The cherry blossoms were in full bloom and Jana glazed into Bruce's eyes, "they remind me of our honeymoon. It was so so very special."

"You are what is so so special to me," Bruce told her.

They got back safely ... but at the airport a smart mouth punk almost met his Waterloo. Bruce steered Jana around him and got her in the taxi. She had no idea what was wrong with Bruce.

"That punk was in prison with me. He is up to no good. If I was not with you, I'd find out," Bruce said.

"Bruce do you know how lucky you are to be out of prison. You have to forget about the agency. I love you. I need you," all five foot of her was angry and he knew it.

When they got home, Madeline and Trevor met them at the door. "Welcome home. How were the folks?"

Jana was still fuming and was polite and went to their room.

Bruce said, "We had a difference of opinion," and he shrugged his shoulders.

"They had a fight!" Madeline told Tate and Debbie that were standing way out of the way.

Trevor says, "It happens to the best of us. We are not going to ever have one of those, are we dear?"

"Not if you play your cards right!" she smiled that sweet smile while rolling her eyes.

Debbie was laughing and Tate still was holding her hand.

"We got something to ask you?" Tate said, "Would it be okay, if Debbie and I took a swim in the pool?"

It was around 8:00 PM and it still was hot and the older couple said, "Help yourself. We are going in where the air-condition is playing our tune. Night to all."

The couple had worn their bathing suits and went into the cabana to leave their clothes while they swam. Debbie held her ring up to the gaslights by the pool as her husband guided her down the steps, and the water rushed over her bikini.

His Speedo fit nicely as she floated up to him, and her arms encircled his neck in one fluid motion.

"You're so beautiful. That wedding ring sparkles as a beacon in the water. I think you really like it," he was stammering.

She had no clue what she was doing to him.

"That bikini is something I wouldn't want you wearing it in the daytime," he kissed her neck.

"Why? Are you ashamed of the way I dress?" she asked.

"It's because everyone could see how much it turns me on!" Tate admitted.

"Oh,!" Debbie was relieved and she smiled."I do believe it does...!"

He couldn't. Couldn't keep his hands off her breast or her buttocks ... Or the dip in her back ...

"This might have been a bad idea, oh wife of mine!"

"Whatever do you mean?" Debbie was rubbing against him because he was turning her on and he didn't want her to stop!

"I'm not going to make it back to the bedroom," Tate was breathing deeply.

"I'll help you!" she said. "Let's go in here."

He was doubled over her as she lay on the cabana sofa. She had slid her bikini bottom off.

He told her, "Don't scream the dogs will eat me alive. Oh! Oh! Everything is already wet!" she closed her eyes and did what he did. She was still learning and learning. He was so gentle and then she became wild, needing it faster. Never had she done that ... and he was losing his mind trying not to scream her name. Then they erupted, the waves took them to the pinnacle! He was holding her tight.

"Tate Tate here it comes again!" He swallowed her tongue.

"Oh baby! Do it like you want to... any anyway you want." She had never done that. He held her afterward gently kissing away the trembling.

"Did I do good?" she asked. "You did great!" he admitted.

"I want to be NORMAL," Debbie smiled.

"This is the normal way two people make love ... not just sex. You are perfect in every way for me!" Tate cuddled her.

They dressed and went back to their room.

"You know when the summer is over I have to decide on a college and you have to make up a year. So think about where you want to live," he was already agonizing over which scholarship to choose. He'd talk to Roscoe. Probably he'd take courses like Roscoe. He didn't want Debbie to ever go back to that school here ... EVER!

"Wherever you want as long as I'm with you. I do love it here at Madeline and Trevor's. They are the best people I have ever met in my life."

"You can just take courses online and be in my bed when I get home. Whatever you want I will back you!" Tate meant it.

Debbie was wiggling up close to his back. "I know you will and I love you. You want to see my ring again?"

"If you don't be still … I'm going to see all of you again!"

"Promises! Promises!" she bantered.

He pulled her close and they lay still.

"You know I love you so much."

"And I … you. Now sleep wife of mine."

"Yes, husband!" and she was grinning.

CHAPTER FOUR

Madeline was getting ready for her mammogram. She hated them. It hurt so bad. The nurses were great. It was that machine that was a torture chamber. It just mashed till you wanted to scream. The test would be read and in two hours, she would see her doctor, Dr. Lee. Her doctor was highly respected in the breast cancer facility and her last operation had been a success.

Trevor was worried because Madeline had been so tired lately. She was keeping something from him and he could feel it in his bones. He flipped the magazine page when she returned.

She had been crying and he asked her, "Did it hurt that bad?"

"Yes and if you got them mashed you'd hurt, too? Let me put yours in a vise, and see how you like it!" Pointing at his crotch and taking a Kleenex out to dab at her tears.

"Not in this lifetime! So don't think about it while I sleep," Trevor crossed his legs and tossed the book on the table.

"We can go eat some lunch. I know you are probably starving. You want cafeteria or junk food?" GM asked.

"Whatever my lady wants is fine with me," he patted her leg and looked around.

"It's mine so I can pat all I want," he laughed so she would cheer up.

"I can see you are worried. We'll see the doctor in a little while. I am here always as you would be for me." Trevor said.

They ate in the cafeteria. She finally told him she had been hurting for awhile, but too scared to make the appointment. She toyed with her food.

"Why didn't you tell me?" he asked. He was concerned to learn that it was not a routine check-up.

"I should have, but so much was happening. The babies ... The trial ... Tate and Debbie, I just didn't feel like stressing you unnecessarily."

"You are my main reason for living. Never keep anything from me," he looked into her frightened eyes.

"You are right. I should have told you. Just all these years I've had to go it alone. My only excuse is a part of me is still independent and stubborn."

"Stubborn as a mule ... but you're still my mule," he was rubbing her hands and kissed them.

"It's time to go and see the doctor," GM said.

"Dr. Lee this is my husband Trevor," Madeline was shaking like a leaf. This female doctor was the best in her field. She had three hundred doctors under her at this university. She was a teacher of the highest quality. It was rare nowadays to find a professional that had a good bedside manner. You could tell, she cared deeply about all her patients. Just observing her making rounds was a delight. Each student was hanging on her every word knowing that she was sharing special techniques, tried and true procedures that only came from many years of experience.

"Nice to meet you," shaking Trevor's hand. Then turning to Madeline. "I knew you were a Smith the last time I saw you, and now a Porter. Congratulations to the both of you. I have read your report and everything looks good on the test. You still look poorly. You say you've been very tired lately. I'm going to order some lab work, if it is okay with you?"

Madeline smiled and said, "Fine. I am so relieved."

They went to the lab and had blood work drawn.

Trevor said, "You really know your way around here."

"I ought to ... I was here for two surgeries and here every day for seven weeks for radiation. They saved my life."

"It's been an hour so we'll go back, and see her again. It's amazing how they send everything from one computer to another. It use to take days to hand deliver x-rays and lab values. Now they just push a button and voila ... it is there."

Madeline said, "We are back."

Dr. Lee said, "Your iron is extremely low. We need to give you an iron injection and a B-12 shot. I'll write you a prescription for iron tablets and have your blood drawn in a month. So make an appointment to see your primary doctor and have him send me the results. You two are a handsome couple. Have a good day!"

"I am going to feel so good soon, you won't be able to keep up with me," Madeline giggled..

"Now that's my girl!" Trevor was so relieved. He was really scared. He could not live, if something happened to her.

The family did not know what was going on with Madeline and Trevor had not told them. He felt it was her place to inform the the "boys" whatever the results would be.

They had called twice and Trevor said, "Honey you really need to ease their minds. If you don't ... I will."

Trevor added, "Maybe tomorrow. It's kinda nice having you all to myself." He escorted her to dinner at the Washington Duke where they were staying. It was magical at night and they strolled outside to the gardens and looked at the golf course.

Madeline asked, "Do you want to stay and play a few rounds?"

"Not this time. You are still fragile. When you feel robust again, we will definitely return to this palace in Durham," he kissed her on the nose and they walked back in where the doorman stood in white gloves and a black tux with tails.

"Oh my ... I could get use to this Trevor," Madeline smiled.

"I guess now you want a butler and a maid," Trevor furrowing his brows and looking sideways at her.

"Only till I feel better," batting her eyelashes at him.

"So be it! I kinda like the idea of you not cooking anymore. Why don't you interview a chef while you're at it!" Trevor said and backed into the room. He knew she wouldn't respond to that in the hallway. He knew she was fixing to blow.

He open the door and when he shut it.

"What don't you like about my cooking?" her chest was rising and falling too fast. Her voice was back to normal and she had her hands on her hips.

"Hallelujah! You are back to normal," he grabbed her and kissed her and held on to her.

"I love everything you do. Your cooking is superb my dear, but ..." Trevor hesitated. "You'll feel better, if you take it easy for awhile," grinning at her.

"What and lie around and do nothing. You have lost your mind Trevor Porter," stripping out of her evening dress and high heels.

"I think you have better things to do than cook every night,"

Trevor kissed the back of her neck.

GM turned around and looked into his eyes, "You just want to have your way with me any time you want to. Right?"

"You betcha I do," and she could not fight it anymore. She melted into him.

"Okay buddy ... you got a deal ... I will pick out a handsome MAN to do my cooking," and winked at him as she went into the bathroom to shower.

"The hell you say!" he followed her in taking his suit off.

"But you just said you wanted me not to cook?" she batted her lashes at him and put her arms around his neck.

"I guess you want me to do the cooking?" grinning at her as they got into the shower of marble and the many jets were angled on them.

"You read me so well my darling!" licking her lips.

"Damn, I got to get me one of those B-12 shots! I think I'm gonna need it soon just to keep " he didn't get to finish before she had blown his thought pattern.

Guy was furious when they arrived home smiling.

"Why did you not return my calls? I have been worried sick!" he was pacing and looking at them.

"Looks like you are okay to me. In fact, I think I'll go have some tests run, if it will make me smile like you two," then he grinned and gave them both a bear hug.

"Yes, the report was good. Just a little low blood that is on the mend. So don't you worry about me," GM kissed her hand and patted GS on the back of his neck. "I'm fine!" looking at Trevor. "He's the one you need to worry about," and she waltzed into the bedroom leaving them both staring.

"What'd she mean by that Trevor?" Guy looked puzzled and then concerned.

"Just means I got to cook for you' all. She has to rest for a while." He shrugged his shoulders. "You are going to have to help me on this one and tell Roscoe I need his help, too! Geez what a mess I am in now."

"What you mean? We'll help," Guy patted him on the back.

"She wants a good looking male chef and I will not hire one!" turning to frown at Guy "You see now what I mean!"

Guy was laughing. "She's playing games with you Trevor. She's going to do the cooking, always has! Did she bat those eyelashes at you?"

"Yep! She did, but truly son she's been sick and keeping it from all of us. She thought her cancer was back and found out it is her iron being low..." he saw Guy's face ashen.

"She has to rest and it will get better. So you and I, and the others, are going to pamper her for a change. Yep that's something we all can do," Trevor was saying.

Tate and Debbie had walked in and heard most of it.

Debbie said, "I would love to cook in that beautiful kitchen, if you will let me, Mr Trevor?"

His knees about buckled, "Would you my dear girl!" He hugged her. Tate was grinning and proud of his bride stepping up to the plate.

"Of course I will. I have been waiting for Mrs. Madeline to give me the okay for awhile now. I just didn't want to barge into her kitchen and take over. I love to cook. I've been cooking for my daddy for years," then she frowned. "He's not talking to me again, but he will eventually. He always does when he sobers up." She couldn't believe she had said that out loud. She put her hand over her mouth.

"It's okay hon," Guy said. "We are family and you can talk to us about anything." He meant it and Tate knew it. They had made them both feel like one of the family for awhile now.

Tate hugged her and confessed, "I have never eaten anything you have cooked. We will do the kitchen work together. Don't you worry, Mr. Trevor. You take care of Mrs. Madeline. She's the sweetest person and we would be proud to help out as much as you 'all have done for us."

About that time Bruce and Jana came to see how Madeline was and over heard the cooking dilemma of Trevor's.

Jana said, "Debbie and I got this. No men needed."

In came Roscoe and the twins, Cain and Caleb ... followed by Kyleigh and Madison.

The women got together and prepared a feast while the men played with the rowdy boys... roughhousing in front of the TV where the football game was on.

Madeline had rested a good two hours when Trevor checked on her. "How you feeling, my love?"

She stretched and he handed her, her medicine which she took and smiled at him.

"I could get use to this, but I had better start supper," getting up from the bed.

"That is my job and it is all done," kissing her ponytail.

Her eyes widened and she stared at him, "I was just kidding earlier!"

"I know you were, but it is about time I took charge of something," and he escorted her to the dining room.

"Something really smells good!" she was still in her robe when she came into the room.

There the family was waiting for her to sit at the head of the table and Trevor at the other end said grace.

"This is so special my children, thank you!" she talked with everyone and found out what had been going on while they were away.

Roscoe said, "The lovebirds, better known as Unitus and Adriana, have gone on their honeymoon to Paris. Otherwise, they would be here for you, too. We are so glad you're home."

CHAPTER FIVE

Chris Shackleford had heard Adam was in the same prison. He'd pay him a visit. He sent word for him to meet him by the weights outside in the courtyard when they were allowed a ten minute free air break.

"Yeah, you botched it!" Chris spit at Adam's feet. "One little bitty elevator and you couldn't even blow it up. What a disappointment!" shaking his head and grabbing a barbell to raise as if he was working out.

Adam sneered "Like you ain't a disappointment to me. Yeah Aunt Eunice told me and I wasn't too happy to learn you were my old man," then he spit at Chris's feet.

They glared at each other. Chris said, "I got the word Tate is living high on the hog these days," still pumping iron and sweating like a pig in the hot sunshine.

Adam became stone-faced, "You leave that boy alone you bastard! Haven't you done enough damage to all of us?"

"Yea yea shut your whinny face ... I hate that family and they are going DOWN ... If it is the last thing I do!" he stood up next to Adam. "You going to help or not?"

"Help kill your ass... sure," bucking up to him with fists high to defend himself.

The guards took them both down and Chris was yelling, "You ain't got the guts to ... you little punk!" dragging him away swinging his arms at Adam.

They took them both and put them into solitary cells.

The guard asked Adam, "Is it true that he is your father?"

"Yeah that's the SOB ... kinda wish he was dead ... but he'd blow his own grave up and come back to haunt me," spitting at the iron bars.

"I'll see if we can't send you to another prison. I'll put in the request today. If he was my father, I'd would want to be far far away from him. Ain't that right?" the guard walked off.

Adam had not answered the guard, but sat staring at the wall digesting what Chris had said about Tate. He would blow his OWN son up to get even with the Smiths!

Chris didn't know about the Porters that had moved in around the bend. Then he laughed. Better to laugh than cry, so Adam decided he would write Tate. Tate had always been talking about this Roscoe. He would protect Tate. Tate could warn that family. That family had done a great thing by taking his little brother in and he owed them. He was so tired of the mess his own life was in, that he wanted Tate to at least, have a chance.

Tate and Debbie had chosen to stay in Hendersonville and go to the college here. With Roscoe's encouragement and a promise of a good job when he graduated, Tate's dream had come true. Debbie said she would go online and finish her few credits for graduation. She then could decide whether to be a stay at home wife or go to college. There were too many grants out there that she would be able to get one, if her grades were good. She was determined to do just that.

Working together, they could do anything.

She looked at Tate, "I know now ... what I want to study. I want to go to culinary school. I love to cook. I truly love to cook," she was hugging him and kissing him.

"Yes Yes Yes" he swung her around. "You are good at it! You are so good at a lot of things!" he was rubbing her back and bringing her close to him.

"Don't you dare ... we are in the kitchen," she twirled away to the other side of the island and was staring back at him.

"Someone might see us!" Debbie said softly.

"We are married Debbie ... it's okay to kiss me in public ... they all do!" he was walking fast around the island.

She was faster and got to the entrance bathroom and she said through the door, "I don't want them to see me all hot and bothered."

"Open this door," Tate was turning the handle. "You had better open this door so they all will not see what you have done to me!" She knew what he meant, and opened the door. Dragging him in fast, she locked the door.

"Now what are we going to do ... we can't get to our room like this?" Debbie asked.

"We can just spend the night in here," he grinned and rubbed.

She could not breathe. He was too close and she could not resist. They were so quiet as they quenched their thirst for each other. Sealing their mouths together so no sound could be heard. In the wee hours of the morning, they came out and made their way to their room.

Adriana and Unitus had touched down at the Charles de Gaulle Airport. They were really here. In Paris, "the city of light," what a special trip this was!

Adriana held Unitus's hand and they walked through the terminal slowly glazing into each other's eyes. Taking a cab to the Hotel de Vendome that was in the heart of Paris.

They were taking in the sights as they rode. He wanted her to not miss a thing. He had been there many times for work, but never had he seen it as beautiful as through the eyes of his wife.

She gushed over the Eiffel Tower in the distance and the green space where the military drills were being held. It was a grand sight to see.

When they arrived at the hotel, Unitus was in full mode of confidence and he showed his bride, the elegant gentleman that she had not seen before. He began to speak to her in French and he escorted her in as the regale lady that she was. She was use to her father's opulence. That ... she had never cared about, but her husband was not showing off. He was teaching her that it was okay to enjoy the riches of their honeymoon. It was for them to enjoy. In French, he was making love to her with his words and she was savoring every syllable.

The hotel was elegant with antique furnishings that would make the faint swoon, but she had been reared in that atmosphere, and it had never appealed to her ... until now.

Seeing her Unitus showing her the hotel, was taking her breath away, and he was controlling himself ... very well.

Until he walked her to their marble en suite and that was where she decided, she would see how much longer he was going to play this perfect gentleman.

She unzipped her sheath and it fell to the floor and she had nothing on, but her high heels.

He stopped and his mouth fell open. "You traveled here with not a stitch under that dress?" His eyes were devouring her as he was taking his clothes off and walking toward her. His eyes staring at her from across the room.

"What am I going to do with you ... You can't travel like that here," he had her in his arms.

"You are going to be the death of me!" he buried his head in her neck and tasted her.

She had not said a word. She didn't have to. He was hers and she would talk later.

They were so spent ... neither of them wanted to go to dinner. The only thing on their minds was to slake their desires till tomorrow. Tomorrow the sunshine would come peeping into their window and maybe they would go out or maybe not. Their needs would let them know. Their main focus was still pleasuring one another from sunup to sundown with no distractions, except "Must feed the baby!" Room service galore with a dessert of prenatal vitamins! "For strength," she laughed plopping the doctor prescribed pill in her mouth followed by her husband's tongue.

"Now that is not what French cuisine tastes like" he laughed.

"Only a baby could like that," he added.

"Aww come here! I'll give you another taste," she had her tongue down his throat and he could not remember what the vitamin tasted like ... nor did he care.

"Oh my wife, you have outdone yourself."

"Oh my husband you have outdone yourself."

They just could not get enough.

"I think we will have to postpone our honeymoon tours until we come again. What do you think Unitus?"

All he could do was moan and ease between her legs.

"Say for me to stop?" she asked.

"I'll never say it!" he made her squeal and she begged.

They were so perfect for each other. "How did I get so lucky, darling?"

"You were working out and I saw your bulging muscle and I could not resist. Remember I was playing it cool ... until you ravished me in the parking lot."

"I beg your pardon, dear ... you ravished me. Telling me here, there, and everywhere I was to take you ...was not something I can EVER forget!"

He rolled her over and looked at her heaving chest, and he kissed her between her breasts. She began writhing against his manhood.

"I woke up every night after that and wanted you so badly."

She said, "You will never be without me ... ever again!"

Two days later, they dressed and went out on a tour of the Champs-Elysees. Then two nights, they stayed in.

Then the following day, they went to the Palais Garnier and saw an opera. She was dressed in her evening dress of cobalt blue and those pale blue eyes were sparkling with mischief.

She gazed at him in his black tuxedo and a bulge was forming as she ran her fingers in his pocket. The lights were dim at the opera and no one could see what she was doing to him. She licked her lips and he was coming unglued.

He just grinned and borne it and said, "Just wait till I get you back to the hotel, my dear."

"Will that be a promise, monsieur?" she teased.

"Oui, Madame!" he winked at her.

They would be going home in one day, so no way were they going to waste it on touring. She was so happy and he was so in love with her happiness. "Will we ever be able to tell our children about our honeymoon?"

He shook his head, "No."

She said, "We had better take a few pictures just for the album. We can get a few pamphlets, and they will never know the difference."

Smiling at each other, they took thirty minutes of pictures and ran back to their room to pack, and ate a parfait, so they could indulge in their lovemaking till the wake-up call in the morning. Then they were off to the airport, and headed home.

Adriana said, "I am glad I was pregnant before I came ... otherwise ... I would be before we got back home."

"Hmm, do you think?" he laughed.

She swatted him.

CHAPTER SIX

The message was for Tate, and it sent a chill up his spine. It was from Adam. The note read:

Watch your back!

Chris is gunning for the Smiths again!

Steer clear. Later!

Adam

Tate called Roscoe and showed it to him. Trevor, Guy, Bruce were called into their powwow.

"This was at least a warning, "Roscoe said. "If it wasn't for Tate, we probably wouldn't know what hit us. Thanks, Tate."

They all patted him on the back.

Trevor said, "He's our family now so that creep doesn't care who he hurts even his own kin. We must think about the women and children and those honeymooners on the mountain will be home any minute. So Bruce, you make sure Unitus knows what we know at all times."

"Yes sir, will do. I have some contacts in the system that will sit on this dude. If you want me to, I can make a few calls?" Bruce added.

"No, you have got to keep a clean nose. Your beautiful wife is looking at you every minute and is frightened. You will not do something stupid like that, not to mention your mother. Not a move from you, sit pat. You can keep your ninjas in place that will help."

"Roscoe have your crew double up until this nut case is squashed. Okay ... I will call in a few favors and have him moved two states over and the warden, my cousin can watch him like a hawk. Anyone else ... any more ideas?" Trevor asked.

All shook their heads negatively, but Guy.

"What about that muffler man named Hal with the pipe bombs?" he asked.

"Geez ... I forgot all about him, Bro!" Roscoe said. "I'll have Inscoe put a tracer on every piece that leaves that shop. If a name comes up twice ... we will be on it!"

"One more thing. Not a word to Madeline. She needs to rest!" Trevor was furious this man had resurfaced. Chris was Madeline's constant nightmare. He was the man that had killed her daughter, Jo Ann.

The weeks that followed were uneventful and the family settled back to a sense of normalcy.

Beatrice was getting big as a house and Roscoe was running himself ragged with the boys.

Guy tackled him with words, "Sit Bro ... You will not like this, but you need a full time housekeeper and a nanny, and I am going to see that you get one or both. I have the money to treat you and Beatrice to this luxury until the twins are born and your football team gets up in age!" Guy was pacing and expecting a fight.

Roscoe was sitting and watching him walk back and forth.

"Sounds good to me!" Roscoe said grinning at Guy.

"You let me go on and on … you weasel," Guy started shadow boxing Roscoe … who was sitting.

Then he arose a good foot taller than him, and Guy frowned. "You just had to spoil my fun. Now sit back down, you look a wreck!"

"If you want to … have Beatrice start interviewing old ladies tomorrow. If she happens to find someone, have them start tomorrow. You look like death warmed over. You are no fun. I want my Bro back! The one that even smiles now and then," Guy was pushing it.

Roscoe showed teeth … A fake smile … Guy knew it well. When he was not happy as a youngster, he would give Guy that same fake smile. The smile right before, he beat his butt!

Guy's eyes got big as saucers, and he was backing up.

"What did I do, Bro?" Guy was asking.

"You have it all figured out. Like you were in an office meeting with a bunch of dummies," he said glaring at Guy. "This is my family and I need to plan out what is best for them all. Yes, a housekeeper would be nice, and a nanny full time, would be wonderful. The one thing missing Bro is … how will my wife feel about this? Ever stop to think that she may not agree with your and my plans? So put the brakes on and I will get back with you. For heavens sakes, don't tell Kyleigh!" Roscoe finished his thoughts.

"OOPS! I talked to her this morning!" Guy was running for the door. Roscoe was chasing him.

"Say you didn't?" Roscoe's lip curled like Elvis's and he had a feeling his night would be topsy-turvy at his house tonight.

Beatrice was in her eighth month of pregnancy and at her wits end. Her hormones were making her cry. When Roscoe would come in and said, "Hello, love!"

The crocodile tears would flow and the hiccups would follow. The twins were walking and into everything. From one thing to another, and the gates were on the stairs, because they were constantly trying to get down them head first.

The chair rail seat had been a life saver for her, but she could only use it when Roscoe was home. Otherwise, the twins would climb the rails, and topple down the stairs, and twice they had been to the emergency room.

"Beatrice did you talk to Kyleigh today?" Roscoe needed to know where her mindset was at this point.

"Yes ... I did and I think it is a wonderful idea." She was smiling at him, but that did not necessarily mean they were on the same page.

He sauntered up to her and took each boy from under her legs where she had cornered them and they were sitting so still.

"Thanks," she had not smothered them. They had just eaten and were ready to sleep.

"Let me put them to bed and then we can talk. I'll be right back." She nodded and rubbed her back. She went and showered and was brushing her long red hair that had grown, and was down her back to her waist. He kissed her neck and she said, "You have got to be kidding. When does the house- keeper and nanny come? Please tell me tomorrow? That is the day you can kiss me all over ... till then don't touch a thing. It may slug you in the face." She grinned and he was going to ...

"I second the motion. Tomorrow will not come too soon!"

He kissed her nape and then her belly.

"My baby is tired. My BeBe has been working so hard on my baseball team that I forgot to take her out to the Ballpark. If that miracle worker comes tomorrow, you and I are getting you out of this house. What do you say?"

"Sounds wonderful. I've done something you may not agree with," she furrowed her eyebrows as if it was painful to say.

OH Lord! Help me! Is what Roscoe was thinking.

"And what's that, my dear?" smiling at her and rubbing her hands.

"I have asked Kyleigh who knows me so well, to pick out the housekeeper and the nanny. I trust her with my life and the life of my children. But YOU, I trust no one with you unless I have the final say. What is your opinion dear?" Beatrice turned her head and looked up at her tall tall husband. He knew he had no opinion except her opinion.

"Sounds about right to me." He stood his tall wife to her full statue and kissed her gently. She took him by the hand and lead him to their bed and said, "Do you want to seal the deal?"

"Of course, my love! I'll turn the baby monitor on and join you in a minute."

"Don't you dare move or the thrill will be gone," she said.

"I understand whatever you say. Oh my goodness!" he said.

The days that followed were planning Christmas festivities.

The shopping even for the sleigh for the horses to pull. It was going to be the Family tradition from this Christmas on, so it had to be grand.

Tate was through with his first term at the college and Debbie had completed her credits and had received her diploma. They both had reasons to celebrate this holiday with thanks. This new year Tate had turned Corey around and his Aunt Eunice was so grateful. They would all be coming to the Porter house to celebrate the season. Corey was bringing a date. He told Tate that she was special. Debbie did not know her, but would welcome her.

Madeline had planned a meal that could only be catered and that's the way Trevor wanted it. Bruce and Jana had pitched in with the decorating. He was smiling as Unitus came through the door with a very pregnant wife. Adriana was still spry on her feet at six months and March 17 was her due date.

Unitus came over and rubbed her belly and talked to St. Paddy. She swatted him. "It's a girl and her name is not Paddy after your old girlfriend." The room roared with laughter.

Madeline asked," Have you decided on a name for her?"

"Courtney or Gym or Adrius or Uranus and the list goes on," her eyes had never left Unitus. He spoke up, "I have a vote for Angel like her mother."

Everyone let out an awwww in unison. He kissed her cheek that was blushing.

Beatrice came in smiling and dressed in an emerald green frock that made her pale green eyes dazzle.

Roscoe said, "Any day now we are going to have a BeBe and a Fifi arriving on the magic carpet ride to the hospital. I pray it doesn't snow this time..." he waved his hands. "But if it does, I have alerted the snowplow man and the highway patrol, just encase. Doesn't she look gorgeous that house-keeper and nanny ... is just what my Beatrice needed." They all applauded his speech and he wanted to add just what I needed, but he didn't. He would have been a dead man of four kiddos, if he had.

He grinned and raised a glass for the toast. "Here! Here!"

Guy had Madison on his shoulders dressed in an elf suit and Kyleigh wore a solid white Vera Wang with sparkling ruby jewelry that was fit for a billionaire's wife.

Madeline wore her red evening gown by Valentino and diamond jewelry as Trevor admired her up close and personal. They had caroling and sleigh rides for all. When the security men were in place, the fireworks went off. They were all the season's colors: red, white, and green bursting in air. Rockets and stars were exploding with bursts of laughter heard, and followed by the merry makers.

Then Beatrice's water broke. Roscoe's face was one of excitement with no comparison, "Christmas presents for me and my wife... have arrived. We just have to go to the hospital and unwrap them." Off they went into the dark of night. She said, "It would be wonderful to see our girls on Christmas Day!" "Yes my love. I agree!" Roscoe always agreed.

PART ELEVEN

CHAPTER ONE

The twins came into the world fast and furious at 11:39pm. Inga BeBe Smith and Roxanna FiFi Smith appeared on this Christmas Day.

"Your mother will have to call you by your name Beatrice, because BeBe and FiFi are our beautiful little girls's names. They will be cute little tomboys though on our baseball team, honey. I can see them now … the remainder of the time, prissy in those princesses' dresses. God I love you," and he kissed her red hair and she fell asleep.

"I know you are exhausted. Sweet dreams my love."

Roscoe sat humming "Silent night, holy night," and rubbing his Beatrice's red hair that always calmed him.

He had talked to Inga and Roberto, Beatrice's parents and he had talked to Madeline and Trevor.

All his chores were done as a new father and he was going to sleep in the recliner by her bed tonight. His boys, Cain and Caleb were asleep, the nanny had said. Tonight they were all at peace.

The TV was still blaring when he woke up … and the movie that GM loved was playing called "White Christmas" starring Bing Crosby …

Beatrice awoke saying, "That is my favorite, too. I've always watched it with my mother every year. I want to get that movie and play it on Christmas Day every year for the girls ... and the boys ... as a family tradition. OK?"

"Anything my Beatrice wants I will try and get!" he was grinning at her. She was an amazing woman, wife and mother.

"How are you feeling?" he asked gazing into her eyes.

She gave him the pout lip and said, "You forgot again!"

"Forgot? What?" he looked puzzled.

"You promised the next time we delivered we were going to have sex all the way to the hospital," she wanted to see what his reaction was going to be. No ways this side of China would she have done such a thing, but they had discussed it in the hospital after the birth of the boys. She sat not cracking a smile.

"Well I ... I mean ... we didn't ... You didn't ask and I am always ready and you mean you wanted to? ... no...I forgot dear... sorry... forgive!" he had been tortured enough.

She smiled and said, "Okay as long as you don't forget next time!" puckering her lips for his kiss.

"Oh My Goodness ... I will never forget again and by the way when do we plan on having this sexual arrival at the hospital, my dear?" kissing her neck.

"Maybe we will rest a year and then have us a set of triplets!" she pressed the nurse's button.

"Quick can someone come and pick my husband up off the floor!" she was trying to scramble out of the bed when several nurses and a doctor came flying into the room.

"What happened?" they were sitting Roscoe up in the recliner and he had a dazed look on his face.

She shrugged her shoulders and played innocent.

"Why don't you ask him?" she was smiling and blowing him kisses.

"She wants to have sexxxxx and tripppletsss," he was staring at the ceiling for divine guidance.

"Is your husband on drugs, Mrs Smith?" the doctor asked.

"No he just woke up from a bad dream and fell out of the chair. She smiled. "It must have been one dilly of a dream! He's still smiling."

"I'd better check and see if he hit his head," he began examining Roscoe.

Beatrice was giggling.

Roscoe said, "She thinks this is funny, Doc. She has a spell on me and there is nothing wrong with my head. She is a temptress and with four children, she asked if we can have triplets next ... I couldn't believe it ... I just I fainted from the stress!" Roscoe still staring at his wife.

She was mouthing behind the doctor with no sound coming out, "I love you."

"Yep! She is really set on triplets so ... I guess we will have to get the show on the road ... Can you good people leave us for a few hours!" He had his back to Beatrice and winked at the doctor.

They all flew out of the room and the mumbling was heard outside the door and halfway down the hall.

Roscoe was grinning and springing for the bed.

"You wouldn't dare?" Beatrice scooted up to the top of the bed.

"You want to bet!" he climbed onto the bed and lay beside her. "No, I will not ravish you, my dear ... but I will if you ever pull that trick again! I could have died. A heart attack... a concussion from hitting my head that bled out ... etc!"

"Stop! I was wrong. I promise not to have sex on the way to the hospital. Okay ... You win! As long as you promise not to leave me with all our children and play baseball without me ... and the TRIPLETS!" She was squealing because he was kissing her so hard.

"Now that's more like it!" she was happy. He was shaking his head and promising while he was holding her in his arms.

They fell asleep and fifteen minutes later. The nurses brought the babies in for their feeding.

Roscoe was not embarrassed and took one of the pink blanketed girls to the recliner to feed her with a bottle. While Beatrice breastfed the other pink blanketed girl.

They were not identical. Bebe had red hair like her mother and FiFi had brown hair like her father.

Roscoe smiled at Beatrice, "I can tell them apart, my darling. Just ask me who's who?" Holding FiFi up to burp her, "I got my FiFi ... she is beautiful!"

Beatrice said, "Yes, just like her ... daddy!"

Roscoe said, "and BeBe is beautiful just like her ... mommy!"

The family came and visited. They oohed and ahhed.

Madison was running and jumping to see the babies ... "Where are their brothers, Mommie?"

Kyleigh said, "They are at Uncle Roscoe's house and we will go see them tomorrow, but tonight we need to see their sisters. Okay?"

Guy had her back,"Madison we could go get some ice cream on the way home and take it to Cain and Caleb tomorrow. What do you think?"

He was clapping his hands. Guy said," Here! Here!' and high fived the little guy. Madison was the spitting image of his father and Kyleigh was blowing kisses as she entered Beatrice's room.

"Hello Hello! How are you feeling my friend?" Kyleigh sat on her bed.

"Hug me gentle … I'm in pain ... but I can't let anyone know, only you will I pour my heart out to ..." Kyleigh hugged her and they talked and talked.

The men were still viewing the girls and Roscoe was passing the taboo cigars out. One of the nurses read him the riot act... "NO TOBACCO ON THE PREMISES!"

She added, "After today!" The stern nurse frowned because she knew the new father tradition was worth a day's grace from the rule because they all promised not to light up.

"Roscoe, she let you by on that technicality when the boys were born. It's a good thing, she's still here!" Guy grinned and chest bumped him.

"Yay! She likes me! She knows, we'll be back, Bro" Roscoe boasted and winked.

Guy gulped, "What are you saying?"

"She already asked … wait for this... for triplets?" Roscoe blew on his knuckles, then rubbed them on his shirt pocket.

"Yep ... got to keep my lady, happy!"

In walks Adriana and Unitus, "I second the motion!" Unitus said rubbing his wife's growing belly which was all in the abdomen. She was fit and with a large sweater, she did not look pregnant. She was an exercise nut and Unitus asked her continuously to slow down.

She would tell him," The doctor said it is good for the baby."

"Two months and we will be in here viewing, My Angel!" Unitus said.

Roscoe asked, "A girl? How sweet! This is the year that the women rule!"

Adriana said, "Yes and don't you men forget it! I am going to meet up with the girls ... Bye proud papa!" and she kissed Roscoe on the cheek.

Unitus quickly popped her on her tush, "Stop that! Not in front of the babies!" She strutted off to Beatrice's room.

"Hey, pretty mama! I brought you some chocolate to cheer you up! The girls are gorgeous!" hugs and kisses followed.

"Wow ... You look great Adriana! Are you eating for two? Doesn't look like it?" Kyleigh asked.

Adriana raised her sweater and there was a cute round belly that she was rubbing the kicking cramp. "She is going to be a kick-boxer ... Wanna feel the strength this kid has?"

"Yep going to be a Pilate's instructor. She's got a wide stretch like her mother …. and a mighty kick like her father," Kyleigh assessed bringing a smile to Adriana face.

"I'm really scared. You two are pros at this. Tell me you two will be there for me. I can't let Unitus know anything or he goes into panic mode," she shook her head up and down.

"We are here for you ... now give me that chocolate!" Beatrice was laughing and eating and Kyleigh was still rubbing the baby's kicking was lessening. "Better?"

"Thanks K … I get pain in my legs and in my back … any remedies?" Adriana asked.

Kyleigh looked at Beatrice and they burst out laughing.

"Well?" Adriana looked at them.

"Wear flat shoes NOT heels … and the legs will be much better," Beatrice said.

"Stop toting all those books and papers around … get a suitcase on WHEELS … your back will feel much better," Kyleigh said.

"You two are spot on … love my girl talk … Now how about the heartburn?" Adriana was grimacing.

Beatrice and Kyleigh looked at each other in unison, "It is nothing you can do about it … it is the CURSE!"

They all three were laughing.

"Thanks I will put you two on speed dial!" she was grinning and they were eating all the box of chocolates.

CHAPTER TWO

The Christmas party had been a success for Madeline and Debbie. Debbie had proven to be a quick learner under Madeline's tutelage. The pastries were heavenly and all had praised her.

Tate was proud of his wife's new talent. His Aunt Eunice had come and Jason had actually behaved. He was amongst other children and he was the oldest. He was delighted in playing with the boys. He was no longer the youngest.

Corey as promised brought his girlfriend, Ellen. Corey was now seventeen and doing well as a senior. Ellen had begun to hang with him at the library when Tate met him twice a week.

Ellen was smart academically and was helping Corey. So Tate was going to taper off to once a week, helping him.

Corey and Ellen walked out back by the swimming pool and were holding hands. Ellen was laughing at Corey's jokes. She was blonde with green eyes, and a mere five foot three to Corey's five foot nine. She was straining to keep pace with his long legs.

"Are you going to a fire?" Ellen asked him.

"No, mom's in there, and I saw this mistletoe. I wanted to bring you out here fast. Just wish I had my skateboard and we'd be here already.

He bent down and kissed her. She was on tiptoe and fell into the kiss. He held her close and raised her high to meet him and then she slid down him.

He said, "We can't do that again." She agreed. It was too intense. Shock was on both their faces. They had been hanging out together and studying, but had never kissed.

It being Christmas was a time to test the waters Corey thought, why not. He had never had a girlfriend and this was new to him. He was going to have to talk to Tate soon!

Sure he had had sex education, but this was the real thing standing in front of him. She was shaking and he should say something so he asked.

"You ever had a boyfriend?" he was looking everywhere but at her, trying to play it cool. He was anxious to hear her answer.

"Nah, no interest in boys. My mother has said time and time again. Boys are trouble. That's all I learned from her till now. I thought that was true. Then you came along." She smiled up at him and now he was looking at her. His stomach was churning and his pulse was racing, yikes now what.

"Guess we better go back in so we don't get into trouble," he laughed and she squeezed his hand. He breathed deeply.

"You are so right about this one Corey. I want to get into trouble with you!" she couldn't believe she had said it.

He stopped her. "What do you mean?"

"I ...I want you to kiss me again," she was blushing as she walked back into the kitchen. Free of his hand and staring at his mother, smiling sweetly. She was searching the room for Debbie. She could talk to her and get some advice.

Madeline had asked her to help Debbie serve the desserts and she was so thankful to be busy.

Trevor had seen the boy named Corey fidgeting and he had asked to speak with Tate. "He has gone to get some more ice. I'm here if you need to talk. I'm a good listener and every-body's grandfather." He smiled and patted Corey on the back.

They walked to the stalls. Trevor remembered Tate saying that his aunt was widowed which meant this boy was fatherless.

Thought you might want to see the horses and get away from the crowd. Sometimes it makes it easier to talk.

"The horses are awesome. Do you let people ride them?" Corey was so excited about the animals here. The dogs were Black Russians and friendly. He began petting them.

"We've never been allowed to have animals where we lived. Mother says it cost too much extra in rent. She couldn't feed them, if she fed us!" He was smiling and talking to Mr. Trevor was easy.

Trevor was nodding as if he knew what Corey was saying was true. He would ask him.

"Mister Trevor I have no one to ask about girls. This girl is a nice girl. She says I am her first boyfriend. She doesn't know that she is my first girlfriend. I don't know what to do?"

"What are you unclear about? Is it sex or real life?"

"Is there a difference? I don't want to do anything that the football team did to my sister! It was not something I would say to anyone. Sorry!" he looked away.

"Are you saying you are afraid to be intimate with your girlfriend? Afraid you may lose it?" Trevor asked.

"I know I want her but I would never hurt her. It is just in the back of my mind, so I freeze when I kiss her." Now he had said it.

"I see your dilemma. Your freezing is the same for every young man. My first love I froze the same as you are describing. It has nothing to do with the football team. They were just evil. Put them out of your mind, son. If this girl likes you, go slow and ask her for permission, and go as far as she will let you."

"You are saying let her make up her mind?" Corey asked.

"If she says no ... then stop. If she wants to go further, then you have to be the man. You say to yourself ... if I get her pregnant, can I marry her? Can I support her? Can I care for a baby?Those are grownup questions I know." Trevor paced.

He continued, "But if it is the right woman for you, you will know. You will know you want to take care of her. You will want to provide for her, and you will want to make love to her for the rest of your life."

Corey shook Trevor's hand, "Thank you, sir! That makes it a lot clearer."

They were walking back and Trevor patted Corey on the back and said, "Anytime you need to talk, I'm here for you."

He hugged Corey like he would any of the kids. Tate saw it and he was glad.

Tate went to meet them. "Corey didn't I tell you he was great," Corey smiled at Trevor.

Then Corey went to find Ellen. He had a new outlook and Ellen did not understand that smile on Corey's face

He was looking at her funny, "Are you sick or do I have something on my face?"

"I will talk about it later. Just know it is important that we work hard this last year of school. I talked to Mr. Trevor and he advise me to talk to you THEN about my plans."

They were at his mother's car and he kissed her deeply.

They were in the backseat when Jason slapped on the window. Thank goodness he always ran way ahead of his mother.

They had felt of each other and were so hot and bothered, but they had only touched. She had not said no. So he had took it to the next level. She was petite, but she was built perfect for Corey. They had fit every part of themselves together with their clothes on. It was a test for both of them.

They straightened and were talking normally by the time his mother got to the car. Neither wanted to look at the other for fear that … that feeling would come back.

Corey walked her to the door with his mother watching. He did not kiss her just said, "good night."

She said, "Call me." He said, "Okay, in thirty minutes."

They talked all night long. Corey was telling her what Mr. Trevor had said.

"He is right about one thing. I want you forever Ellen. You may not feel the same and I need to know that now?"

"I want you Corey, too. Did you not feel my panties?" she asked.

"Did you feel how hard I was for you?" he asked.

"I did and I want you, too. We have to think smart. It's our senior year!"

"The problem is I have to get condoms or you have to get on the pill. We will never make it to June with you talking like that to me."

"Corey, I am on birth control pills ... since I was sixteen, mother insisted. I haven't seen anyone I wanted until you."

"You said what? You are on the pill? I love you!" Corey said it finally.

"You said what? You love me? Where did that come from?"

"I have known it for a while, but did not know how you felt until you said you wanted me."

"Corey I want you to be the first!"

"I want it everyday ... sorry I got carried away ... I have to focus ...," he said.

He grabbed the skateboard and out the door. His mom and Jason were still sleeping. When she saw the board gone, she would think he was skateboarding with the guys.

He was still on the phone with Ellen and it was 7:25 by his phone clock. "I am going to see you in ten minutes."

He was rounding a curve and almost missed his turn. He stopped and turned his body to the sign post as her mother passed him in a hurry.

"I just passed your mother. Are you in the garage?" he said into his phone.

"Yes and I will flip the switch and let you in!" she did.

He whizzed under the door and grabbed her with one motion and had his hands in her sweats holding her buttocks and kissing her neck. His board crashed up against the wall.

She had mashed the button for the door to close as he came under. She was kissing his neck and her arms were around his neck.

"Ellen you are so perfect and petite in my hands, and I know I don't want to be rough with you," he was begging her to understand.

She stripped her top off and he stripped his sweatshirt off. They lay naked and felt all the parts that they had felt in the car, except this time they were making a visual massage to their soul ... the massaging intensified.

She whispered in his ear, "Oh I love you so much!"

That was all the restraint he had, "I love you, too!"

"Will you marry me?" he asked.

She answered, "Yes!" He kissed her softly.

He said, "You know I have to go, but there will be a day I will never have to leave you."

She waved, "I know you have to go. Be careful."

"I'll call you when I get there." He kissed her and skateboarded home. He was going to get a job in the afternoon and get a motorbike. No way could he afford a car. He was going to talk to Tate, and see if Roscoe had any type of job that he could do in the afternoons.

CHAPTER THREE

Roscoe gave Corey a job sweeping and mopping the bathroom on all three floors of his security office building. Two days a week Tuesdays and Fridays.

Ellen was not a happy girl until he told her, it was to get them a means of travel. Then she smiled and kissed him in front of the office building which made Corey blush because everyone was looking at them. Tate walked them to the college library and said. "I see I am no longer needed as a tutor. Ellen make sure he does his homework or my wife will be upset with me for letting Corey down."

She smiled sweetly and said looking at Corey, "I will give him all the homework, he can handle. Don't worry Tate, he's a fast learner."

Corey dropped the mop and Tate almost split his sides laughing as he jumped in the car to ride home with Roscoe.

"Guess I need to get a job to get a set of wheels," he told Roscoe.

"And where would you drive, but to the same places the family goes everyday. Right? Put your money in the bank if you decide to get a job. I hope you don't, I want your grades to be so good that you go to that school Guy went to."

"Yeah I heard he is opening GM & GS Private Investigation Service back up. He may need some help," Tate was excited at the prospect of working for Guy.

"Why don't you give him a call?" Roscoe hummed all the way home to see his boys, after he dropped Tate off.

Beatrice and the girls were not home yet. He would shower and play with them for an hour and off to the hospital, he would go.

"Tomorrow," Beatrice said as Bebe suckled her breast and Roscoe was feeding FiFi her bottle of breast milk.

"I am so glad ... I have missed your mama in my bed, FiFi," he was burping her now, and making goo goo eyes at her mother.

"Tell me about your day, darling? You smell so good. Did the nanny make eyes at my handsome husband?" she was patting and burping BeBe, and smiling.

"Of course, she did dear! She's as old as GM. She is always making eyes at me. Do this, do that ... geez I will pay Kyleigh back for that one!" Roscoe frowned.

Now Beatrice was a happy woman and said, "She did what I asked her to do! No payback for my dearest friend, unless you want to buy her a diamond necklace. I will help you pick it out for her. I know what she likes," grinning like a Cheshire cat.

Madeline and Trevor walked in after knocking, "We just had to see those beautiful girls of yours."

"You coming home any time soon Beatrice? I talked to the nanny and she looks a little bit worse for wear," Trevor asked.

"Honey, sweetie. Can I stay for a couple more days?" Beatrice asked Roscoe.

"You can, if I can stay too. Just ask the doctor, dear. I have no authority here," Roscoe smiled sweetly.

Looking at Trevor adding, "Or at home."

Trevor nodded and Beatrice threw a pillow at Roscoe and he caught it.

"Sweetie, we have company ... Relax. I'll ask the doctor."

Madeline said, "You are in deep trouble son and I know you are kidding, but the nurses are forming sides, and they may keep you on another floor here!"

They all burst out laughing and the girls heads were turning and looking at their parents as if to say what is that noise these grownups are making. It is called laughter.

Roscoe was rocking and laughing for FiFi, and Beatrice was cooing at BeBe.

In comes Kyleigh and Guy with hugs and kisses for the babies. Roscoe, "Hey over here ... do I look like chopped liver? I need one of them."

Instead of them hugging and kissing him, Beatrice got out of the bed and planted one on him.

"Oh my goodness! I was not expecting that ... but I sure did like it. Can I have another?" Roscoe asked.

"He likes to ask for more!" she had a twinkling in her eye.

He wobbled and Guy caught his arm and sat him down.

"Now Now Beatrice! He is a new father. You might have hurt him. Get the doctor, Kyleigh!" Guy teased.

Trevor said, "You two boys had better stop before one of these nurses takes you serious!"

In walked the nurse, "Nah Mr Trevor, we remember these two from the twin boys' birth. I'm use to them by now ... Just heard you are having triplets next time ... so come closer. On the way to the hospital, here's my NUMBER send me a text. I can call in and request a week's vacation," she was grinning.

Then she slapped Roscoe on the sleeve, "Just kidding … I wouldn't miss it for the world," and she held up three fingers.

Roscoe almost fainted again. Madeline ran to him, "Are you alright son? Has your blood sugar dropped again?"

"No ma'am, I checked it earlier when the missus made him faint for real!" said the nurse.

Beatrice was avoiding Madeline's stare and humming to the little BeBe.

"Okay you two what happened?" Madeline asked.

Beatrice pretended to zip her lips sealed. Trevor was killing himself laughing as was Guy.

Kyleigh took FiFi from Roscoe.

Roscoe stood beside Beatrice and like he was reciting the Gettysburg Address said, "My beautiful red haired wife announced to the world that we are having TRIPLETS next time, but she failed to disclose what she said before that… that caused my knees to buckle. Yes I did, indeed, hit the floor!" pacing. "I admit I cannot divulge what she said. I would like her … to tell you all herself," and he smiled at her and kissed her hand and rushed across the room to the other side.

Everyone was looking at Beatrice and waiting … and waiting. She was turning red in the face and Roscoe was hiding behind Madeline peeking at her.

Guy whispered to Roscoe, "You are dead meat tomorrow!"

Roscoe said, "I know I can hardly wait!" there was a twinkle of excitement in his eyes.

Kyleigh said, "Stop it you two! She is going to cry!"

She rushed to Beatrice and huddled over her, "Pretend to cry, love … that will teach them a thing or two."

She sobbed into Kyleigh's shoulder, "Is it working?"

"Like a charm … continue," she patted Beatrice on the back.

Beatrice whispered in the huddle, "You are so smart that's why you are my best friend. I owe you one."

"You'd do it for me!" Beatrice peeped at Roscoe, he was petrified.

"He is not petrified that I am crying. He is petrified what I will do to him tomorrow for embarrassing me. Let him stew!"

"He may faint again?" Kyleigh mouthed.

"You are right…" Beatrice said.

"Roscoe I need a hug!" She said softly.

He went running, "Coming, dear!" she whispered, "I love you to death do us part!" His eyes dilated he thought she is going to kill me. His mouth was open.

Guy came over to stand beside Kyleigh and said, "Shut your mouth Roscoe!"

"What a mean thing to say," said Madeline.

"It's not Madeline, the boy is drooling," Trevor added.

They all laughed loudly … all the nurses came running.

"We missed something. I just knew it soon as I left …" the older nurse said. "You just got to love this family, I do!"

The dogs had been barking and barking. Tate and Debbie, and Bruce and Jana were in the living room watching a movie. Someone was out there.

There was a knock at the door and the honeymooners waltzed in carrying gifts from Paris.

"Not much but we wanted you all to have an Eiffel Tower."

Adriana and Unitus smiled at one another. They had bought a case and had them shipped home before they left Paris.

"We had very little space in our luggage for big items," Adriana said which was true. It was the time thingy that made them pick the one item. She didn't even like to shop for clothes.

Jana grinned the most, "This is perfect who doesn't love the Eiffel Tower? It's the first thing you think of when you think of Paris, thank you both." Unitus was busy patting her on the head and measuring Jana's height, she swatted at him.

Bruce said, "I have to tell you two lovebirds something and I don't want to forget. "While you were gone we had a scare, do you want to tell them Tate?"

Tate told them of the letter his brother had sent. Unitus was gritting his teeth. Something Adriana had never seen before.

Adriana asked who this Chris Shackleford was? And Madeline heard that as she came through the door.

"What about that monster have you all been keeping from me?" She turned to look at Trevor who was hanging his coat up and intentionally not looking at her.

"Well Trevor Porter lay it on the line?" she stood with her hands on her hips facing him. No one moved.

Adriana knew this was serious and the baby was kicking so that she sat by Unitus and grabbed his hand. She laid his huge hand on her belly, so that the baby could kick him for awhile.

His face was angry, he must know of this man. He was rubbing her stomach gently and calming the baby. She was calming her husband by rubbing his back.

Trevor turned, "You were sick and feeling poorly. I didn't think nor did the boys think that we should worry you with this."

Unitus whispered in Adriana's ear, "This man killed Madeline's daughter years ago." She gasped, but it gave her insight into the intensity of the situation.

"So the boys knew, too. I will deal with those two later. Go on my dear husband," and she took her coat off and folded it over her arm.

Tate and Debbie had coward to the rear and would be ready to flee, if need be.

"Tate got a letter that Chris was going to take the Smith family down and that his brother Adam wanted Tate to warn us. If Tate were not here, Lord knows what would have happened. They have moved him to my cousin's prison and he is in solitary confinement. There is no need to worry. Roscoe has double security around the clock and Bruce here has his ninjas, also guarding the place. I just felt we should notify Unitus and Adriana, encase they saw or heard something to call us or Roscoe. I have the dogs trained in all three houses so I want Unitus for your house to have a dog also. My dogs are Black Russian Terriers, and trained to rip a man apart. If a woman is held down and she screams, and if it is something bigger than that … they will press the installed button … the SBI and FBI will come as well as the local law enforcement. I have covered all the bases, honey. Unless now that you are feeling better, you can think of anything else?"

"I am feeling better, but I am mad as hell and you know it, Trevor." She hung her coat up. "For you that don't know, I was the private investigator who put Chris Shackleford behind bars. I have run the best agency in these areas for ten years. All of a sudden … I am not to know anything when my family is in jeopardy. Shame on you Trevor."

He knew she was mad and had a right to be. He should have told her. He just loved her too much. So all he could do was nod and pace.

"Wait till I get my hands on Roscoe and Guy," now she was pacing.

"Honey, Guy has his hands full with Kyleigh, if she hears she will freak out, and Roscoe lord knows has his hands full. Would you not say? Take it out on me, my love."

She turned and went to Tate and hugged him and Debbie who were stoned face. She herself knew first hand about fear of mean people that wanted to do harm to you.

Adriana had dealt with the lowlifes in the court system but had never faced personal fear, and did not with Unitus beside her. She felt safe. He had been training for a triathlon. He had mastered the swimming and the blade running and was trying to perfect the cycling transfer. He was her hero in every way. She felt safe with him by her side and smiled at him.

"I forgot. We also have Hal's Garage under surveillance. This is the tricky one. He is the pipe bomb dude that makes homemade bombs and ships them in tailpipe parts boxes. We have not been able to catch him. Only reports come in from street talk and hearsay. So that one, we put a undercover agent in his shop."

"That is why Guy wants to ... all of a sudden reopen GM & GS Private Investigation Service. Isn't it?" looking at Trevor.

He shrugged his shoulders to keep from saying it.

"Well I am going to take my IRON tablets and get a good night's sleep. See you 'all in the morning. Goodnight!" and she went to her room.

"I'm going to talk to her. You 'all make yourselves at home Goodnight!" he was going slowly to their master suite.

CHAPTER FOUR

Jana looked at Bruce, "I know what you are thinking. But I beg you not to."

"This is what Unitus and I do ... we take out the bad guys," Bruce was pacing in their bedroom.

"That is what you did when you had the agency behind you. You cannot make one false move or you are sent back. I love you. I want you here with me," Jana pleaded.

"It is my family. Your family. I can't sit back and do nothing for heaven sake, Jana!" Bruce breathed deeply.

"Then talk to Guy, Trevor, and Roscoe and see if you can do anything within the law. For goodness sake Unitus is needed at home. His wife will give birth in a month and he should be here with her! You should be here to help protect her and me ..... and here to protect Unitus. You promised him."

That rang a bell for Bruce. Unitus had always protected him on all their missions together, and he did need to do that.

"You have to protect your grandson." That also rang a bell. Jana knew how to ground him.

"You are right yet again, that's why I love you so much, my Jana. Guy may need me in his new business. Wouldn't that be and about face? Adriana is looking at Unitus with worry in her eyes. I will talk to him," Bruce vowed.

"I think he is angry at anyone who'd try to hurt any of us and afraid that Adriana may get caught in the crossfire. I will talk to her when you talk to Unitus," Jana said and nodded.

Guy had not rode his bike in a long time, but it would be quick transportation to the office with his shingle was on it, and free up the car for Kyleigh and Madison to do their visiting and shopping.

He zoomed down to see GM and get the key and her blessing. She was in the kitchen patting her foot and hands on her hips.

"OH BOY! What have I done now?" Guy was perplexed. He could not think of a thing.

"Is it the bike?" he asked grabbing an apple to bite. Best stay busy when grandma is patting her foot. She is ready to rumble. He hadn't eaten breakfast, so he was grabbing a cinnamon bun, too.

"You know what I have not been told. Sit before you choke on something!" GM said.

She poured a cup of coffee as Trevor rounded the corner and his eyes were rolling, and he shook his head up and down while Madeline had her back to him.

Guy made a horrible face of misery, then straightened as Madeline turned and caught them both making FUN of her anger.

"You two think this is so funny, but I don't!" she fumed.

"No ma'am. I … We just didn't want to worry you. Now now pat my neck and say you will help me open up our office today?" GS asked with those puppy dog eyes.

She kissed her hand and swatted the back of Guy's neck as Trevor winked at Guy and gave him the okay sign.

"She's taking those iron tablets so watch out Guy, she's made of steel now!" and grinned. This would keep her out of the house worrying him. He had the office set up with his networking and he didn't want her prying into it. He was keeping that door locked because he had a pulse on every family member."

Tate was off to school and kissed Debbie bye, as Roscoe stopped to pick him up. Debbie asked Madeline, if it was anything she could do for her?

"No dear, but I will be gone with Guy to the office and just call me, if you need me. You can have free rein of the kitchen. Experiment all you want," Debbie hugged her.

"I do have a test at the college. I have to present a homemade dish of my own creation and give an oral presentation to the class. I need to practice really bad," she said as she ran to her room.

"Trevor make sure she doesn't burn the house down," Madeline said as she jumped on the back of Guy's bike.

"Guy be careful with my wife on the back of that thing. Madeline honey, I can drive you!" Trevor frowned.

She was waving and Trevor was angry. "That's why you wore those jeans and cowboy boots ... I guess I will have to get her a three wheeler!" he was mumbling all the way back to the house. In the kitchen, he saw Bruce and Jana getting coffee and he spat out, "Did you see what your mother left on? She is going to give me a heart attack one of these days!" His face was so red. He was still mumbling under his breath.

"Trevor you do remember that she and granddad use to ride Harleys every weekend?" Bruce reminded him.

"Yeah, but that was twenty years ago. She's no spring chicken," Trevor was laying it on the line. His fear of her getting hurt was on his mind big time.

"Trevor you had better never, I mean never! Let GM hear you say that or you will be sleeping in the doghouse," Bruce said looking at Jana that was nodding that he was right.

"Bruce have you seen the dogs' house out back? It is fit for a KING, so I will take my chances." He went off to his office.

Bruce said, "I think I will go up and see Unitus while Adriana is at work, then we can maybe meet them for a night out at THE INN?"

Jana said, "Sounds good to me. I'll stay and help Debbie with her cooking assignment. I can video her and she can see what she needs to work on for class."

He left walking up the mountain. One of his ninja employees walked with him. It was Jana's cousin, Haruto. His brother was on watch at night and his name was Minato. Bruce could tell them apart by their voice and with his own face staring back at him. He asked, "Haruto take the mask off when you are with me. Have you met Unitus?"

"No, he has no idea who we are under these masks and that is okay! As long as that big man doesn't come after me, I won't hurt him!" They both laughed.

"I will introduce you to him, my friend," Bruce said.

"If that is your wish," he bowed to Bruce. Bruce stopped and bowed to him. They both respected one another.

Haruto was grateful for his job. It had provided for his family to live well back in Japan. He had brought his wife to America, and she was staying with him at the Best Western

145

outside of Hendersonville. Her name was Machi and her sister Mitsumi had come, also.

Mitsumi was in love with Haruto's brother, Minato.

Minato worked the night shift for Bruce. He was a brown belt master in judo. He was not the marrying kind, Haruto told Bruce. "But you know women … they can change our way of thinking … if they put their minds to it."

Bruce laughed, "Don't I know it! Your cousin has me wrapped around her little finger." He walked a few steps and added, "Don't repeat this Haruto … but I'm hen-pecked!" He raised his chin and smiled as they got to Unitus's door.

Haruto said, "Not me! Your secret is safe."

Unitus said, "Come in … who do we have here?"

Bruce said, "You know him…" He nodded at Haruto who put his Bruce mask on.

"Oh I do know him. He could be your twin," Unitus smiled.

"Haruto is Jana's cousin and has been working for me for many a year on our missions in Japan. I wanted someone reliable here for us to protect our family. I wanted you to meet and his brother is here at night. They are our allies, if we need them. This with Chris Shackleford has everyone on edge, but Trevor he has faith in his cousin the warden."

"I trust no one but my friends!" Bruce admitted.

Unitus shook Haruto's hand and he bowed giving a small smile to Bruce. "I'll be going back to my post, but I would like to know a sign, if you need help Mr. Unitus?"

"It will be a Tarzan yell," Unitus told him.

Haruto looked at Bruce for clarity.

Bruce told Unitus, "Unitus do it! He has no idea who Tarzan is … Go on and show off."

Unitusbellowedthefamous, "AAHAAHAAAHHHHH!"

Haruto's eyes got big, "That's a good one. I will tell Minato! Good day!" he bowed and put his mask on, then vanished into the woods.

"Just wanted to touch base with you. Jana has read me the riot act. Your sweet wife got me another extension. If I fart wrong, I'll go straight back. So I was enraged as you at the thought of someone harming our family. You cannot try anything either. That wife of yours is going to pop any day now, and you will have to stay put on this mountain."

"Yes! I got the riot act last night, too. They are professionals you know. They just peck away at us, don't them?" they laughed and hugged.

"And we love it. Unitus, do you ever remember us not having them by our sides? I can't go back. You have to stop me, if I ever freak out again." He lowered his head into his hands, "I am so blessed to have you as my friend."

"Always, the women get along, too … so that's good. What are they plotting now?" Unitus asked.

Bruce admitted, "To go to dinner at THE INN! Want to?"

"When have I ever refused food? These workouts make me want to eat a horse. I have been eying Trevor's all day!"

"You know that's dangerous!" Bruce said.

"I know eating is my downfall. I just have to. To keep up my strength…" Unitus said frowning.

"Training can make you hungry. It is natural, but those horses are thoroughbreds." Bruce nodded.

"The training is not what I have an appetite for. It's trying to keep up with Adriana … she is a thoroughbred times ten!" He was grinning at Bruce as if he had swallowed a canary.

"You braggart!" Bruce sneered.

"Yep … Just don't know how I got so lucky? She is so happy about the kid. You haven't seen the nursery? I know she showed it to Jana … so let me show it to you."

Unitus was on a cloud. Bruce had never seen him so happy. The room had white furry bunny rabbits, and of porcelain, wood, and glass. Also a really nice collection of Boyd's bunnies on a white shelf over the white changing table with glass knobs on the drawers. "WOW!"

The comforter was of pink gingham with white eyelet lace trim and matching bumper pads, and a white cashmere crib blanket. The mobile had the cow jumping over the moon and sheep that bounced as it turned to the tune of "Somewhere over the Rainbow" sung by Judy Garland.

"The walls were a pale blue like Adriana's eyes and the rocker-gliders were cobalt blue like his..." pointing to his eyes. There was a sparkling diamond chandelier hung from the ceiling and vintage posters of doll babies of yesteryear …

Unitus said, "The white rocking horse has a mink mane and a soft tanned leather saddle with matching leather bridle."

He shook his head, "Yes! her father sent it and the portrait of Adriana dressed in a big hat, long beads with over sized high heels on, and she was the age of THREE. That's the one hanging at the top of the baby's bed. Guess next, the old man will send a silver spoon to feed her with … Don't get me wrong. I think it is wonderful because it makes my wife squeal when she unwraps stuff." He paced the room.

"Bruce I want to be the only one that makes her squeal."

"TOO MUCH INFORMATION!" Bruce laughed.

Unitus was talking more than Bruce had ever heard him talk in his whole life. Adriana had brought the best out of him.

The girls came into the nursery and Adriana asked, "Too much information about what, Bruce?"

Unitus hugged her and said, "About our love life dear!"

She swatted him, "You wouldn't dare?" "No but," he knelt and kissed the baby. "Hello little one I have missed you all day long!" He looked up, "I bet you and Jana tell each other ... tell all!"

Bruce's eyes turned to Jana, "You wouldn't dare?" mocking Adriana.

Adriana said kicking off her high heels, "You all are clearly low on blood sugar ... and your brains are not functioning at full capacity, so let's go eat! I"

Walking out barefooted, "I am eating for two you know, and have been kicked for the last hour ... as if she is saying FEED ME ... mama!"

They raced to the van and Unitus drove down the hill like a pro.

Bruce said, "That training you are doing has you in good shape, bro." He was amazed how fast Unitus had become.

"I have to be ... encase my woman wakes up and says ... It's time to go to the hospital. Been practicing. Practice makes perfect!" Unitus said rubbing Adriana's leg.

"Okay I was talking about the triathlon so keep both of those hands on the wheel." They all burst out laughing.

"You guys can drink tonight, but neither of us can," Adriana showed the pouty mouth.

"It's okay … we will suffer through it. Unitus likes being a designated driver. He won't even let me drive," Adriana shared.

"That's because your belly will not fit behind the steering wheel without Angel having her head rubbed," Unitus teased. They had their seats at the finest private dining room by then.

Adriana said, "His head may need rubbing!"

Unitus said, "Don't talk like that in public darling!"

Jana said, "I'll have … what they are having!"

Bruce looked at her, "I think my head needs rubbing after being with these two!"

Jana grabbed him under the table, "Behave!"

Bruce was staring at her, "I will … if you promise."

"I promise," Jana said blowing him a kiss.

He gulped. Unitus looked at Bruce, "You are so pecked."

Eating his steak, "Takes one to know one!"

Jana and Adriana were eating their salads and making faces at the men.

Only Adriana had a habit of putting her feet in Unitus's crotch, so he could rub them at night.

He said, "Not now honey!" and kept eating.

Bruce had to ask, "What does she want?"

Unitus said as he finished eating his baked potato, "To have sex on the table," the waiter almost passed out.

"I am kidding mister, don't throw us out!" Unitus was smiling at Bruce that was having a hard time containing himself.

Adriana said, "Tell him buster, if you want to live till we get home."

"Okay Okay! She likes me to rub her feet while we are eating. She has been in heels all day and says it relaxes her. Happy Angel."

"Happy ... you are finally doing it! " she blushed.

"Just wait till I get you home," Adriana said.

The waiter and another employee were talking. One said, "You know that is the mean district attorney uptown! I bet she has a black whip that she uses on him every night!"

"Do you think that is why his arms are so swollen?" the other waiter said.

Bruce walked by going to the bathroom and said, "Nah, he's a body builder and he can pick the both of you up at the same time and throw you up against that wall. So I really would advise you not to be talking about his wife like that, where he might hear you!"

They were quiet as church mice the rest of the evening.

"Any dessert?" the waiter asked.

Unitus said, "None for me, I'm watching my figure."

Adriana looked at the ceiling, shaking her head, "None for me either. I am watching his figure, too!"

Bruce and Jana lost it! They all left laughing all the way to the van.

Jana said, "This is what we have been needing. We must do it more often. Bruce agreed, "It was wonderful. Night all."

"Anytime!" as they dropped them off before going up the mountainside.

CHAPTER FIVE

Madeline and Guy had made peace when they saw the shingle on the building, GM & GS Private Investigation Service. She opened the door and it was like old times. They started reorganizing and discarding things that were out of date and began tracing the leads they had had on Chris in the past. Old contacts that they had in the computer database. They didn't want to miss a thing.

"LEAVE NO STONE UNTURNED," The old plaque still was hung on the wall and she ran a finger across it.

"I remember when you burned this into the wood at wood shop, and gave it to me for my birthday. It is still special to me ... as you are," GM said.

She blew him a kiss and GS caught it and slapped it on the back of his neck.

They heard someone on the porch. He looked, "It's Trevor." He probably doesn't want you to ride home on the bike. Yep I do believe the man has been shopping.!"

She ran to the door and swung it open and her eyes dilated at the sight of a Tri Glide Ultra by Harley-Davidson. He said, "You want to ride a bike, then you're going to ride it with me. So get on my lady and I will ride you home."

"Oh My Goodness what have we here? It is a trike, but it is beautiful!" It was black and shining with chrome and the seat was so soft and comfortable, not like that dang thing Guy has.

Trevor was sitting tall in the saddle. "Hold on woman!"

She grabbed his waist which was not necessary to do on this machine, but she was hugging him for his thoughtfulness.

This was going to be her transportation to and from the office. He just didn't know it quite yet. Or did he? Hmm.

"The limo is never going to be used Trev!" her ponytail was whipping in the wind.

"I know only on rainy days," he laughed. She would tire of this he hoped, and he could give this thing to Tate and Debbie. Till then, he was going to enjoy Madeline being back to her old feisty self.

Guy walked through the door and Madison was running for him. "He is not use to you being gone all day!" Kyleigh was batting her eyelashes at him.

"Oh boy looks like someone else missed me, too!" she wiggled her new skinny jeans at him.

"You betcha!" Kyleigh was backing up.

"Take them off!" He grinned.

"Not in front of Madison," who was not paying them any attention because he was building a fort.

Guy tackled her and she landed on the couch and he on top of her.

She said, "You see that beautiful dog sitting over there. He's this close ..." She spread her fingers one inch apart. "He is going to bite your arse and you will be home with me all day for awhile!" She was wiggling and he was hardening.

"You wouldn't dare? Be still. I have decisions to make." Guy was looking at her dog and smiling.

"Come here baby and give mama a kiss," here comes the dog and Madison. He knew she would not scream and he was working her into a fevered pitch with his hands and finally he said, "take them off now!"

He told, "Velvet watch Madison," and he took Kyleigh into the small bathroom beside the dog.

He was willing to get bitten to slake his thirst for his wife and she was just as needy. They couldn't help it. Nothing could stop them once it got started.

He had promised himself … if she ever recovered from her kidnapping, he would make sure she would be loved every chance they had. No matter where they were or what they were doing, she was his number one priority.

"Oh baby you are so good to me. I may go to the office everyday, if this is my reward."

She peeped through the door. Madison was still playing and the dog was right beside him. "What the heck … I think you have more for me?" and she wiggled.

"I'll always have more if you do that! We may never leave this room." Madison was knocking on the door, "Mommie… Daddy … Peep a boo!"

They were taking turns opening and shutting the door, and they never stopped their rhythm.

He sealed her mouth so no scream came out as she climaxed.

"MARRY me again? I love this! Ours is heaven on earth, and no one knows what it can be like unless they have a partner made so perfect as you are for me."

She said, "Here! Here!" the Smith toast.

She washed and was starting to put those jeans on. "Give them to me, or suffer the consequences," she handed them to him.

"Okay I'll just walk around naked, the security should enjoy that," he frowned and handed them back to her.

She wiggled into them.

He picked up Madison and rubbed the dog's head.

"See your mother tempting your father ...what am I saying. We are going for a walk Madison," he told the dog to stay.

He wanted that dog between them and to protect her from him the rest of the day. When night falls, the dog will be in his crate asleep and the baby will be in his crib, she will pay if she still has those skinny jeans on.

She had her pre- pregnancy shape back, except her boobs were huge. Yep those were Madison's now. He has got to stop this daydreaming and watch were he was ... Madison was jumping and giggling. "Daddy Daddy catch me."

He jumped from the swing set and they both landed in the sawdust. They roughhoused for awhile and then brushed off. Guy saw movement in the bushes. He got on his cell phone and called security to see if they saw anyone southeast of their house.

"Negative sir," they were quick to respond. That was reassuring after today at work, he was on edge. Then a deer poked his head out and came into the open space to graze.

"Madison shh," and pointed to the deer. The boy stood still with his mouth open. His son loved nature. "Deer ... daddy can I ride him?" he thought everything could be rode.

Beatrice was finally home with the girls, and Nanny Brice was organizing everything while Roscoe was settling

Beatrice in their bedroom. She had kissed the boys and they were involved in building a fort in the den, so they had little time for mommy.

Roscoe was beaming at her, "You want to rest or make babies?" She threw a pillow at him and he said, "I guess that is a no."

"I'll just go see to the boys while you take a nap," he quickly darted out of the room.

Mrs Boomingdale was cleaning the hallway and asked what they wanted for supper. The twin boys said in unison "Hot dogs!"

"And you sir?"

"The same will be fine with me, but her royal highness may want something special! Please ask her when she wakes, and if we don't have it, I will go get it. Okay? Thanks Mrs B, you are an angel." He was grinning at her.

The sarge would straighten Beatrice right up or we will be missing one good housekeeper and cook.

He crossed his fingers behind his back as he looked out at Guy's. There was Madison and they were looking at a deer. So he ran to get the twins. He drove slowly, but the boys were making too much noise, over excitement to see the deer had won and it ran away.

The boys piled out and ran to see their cousin. Now the three boys were almost three. Rambunctious as ever, the yard had the most play equipment and they would sleep good tonight, "Let them play and we can talk and catch up." They sat in the chaises by the fire pit and watched the boys.

Kyleigh brought them all a cooler on a wagon, full of homemade lemonade, and disposal cups with lemon slices.

Guy was eying her skirt. She had changed to calm her husband's libido while they had company.

He was following her with his eyes begging. She was still smiling when she left.

"Stop it Guy! You are acting like a man in heat. It is me that is lacking. I mean really lacking these days," Roscoe said.

Guy sipped his lemonade and said, "The more you get the more you want! BESIDES you have four kids so I know you have not been lacking at all."

Roscoe shook his head up and down, "Ain't that the truth! Yes four times a day to make those girls! " smiling and Guy was stunned.

"Geez that's what I being doing wrong, I quit after two times today!"

Roscoe crossed his legs together and showed some teeth. "You just had to say it. Rub it in, Bro. You are so cruel. If you mess with me, I'll give you a knuckle sandwich."

"What are Brothers for!" patting Roscoe on the back.

The twins ran to ask their daddy, "What is a knuckle sandwich? I'm hungry!"

Madison was right behind them. "I'll ask mommy to make some knuckle sandwissshes!" Cain and Caleb were cheering.

When they got home, Beatrice was dressed in skinny jeans. Except her legs were a mile high, and Roscoe was drooling.

He started assessing her change from hospital gown to sexy attire, and that red hair all pulled up on top of her head and dang makeup!

He was in for it. "Down boys!" and he wasn't talking to the twins, but they thought he was and they sat down.

Both were staring up at their mommy and daddy, looking from one to the other.

Roscoe could not stop staring at her even as Mrs B came and got the twins to feed. The dog was trotting behind them, and Roscoe locked the door.

"You look ravishing. I think I will go shower before dinner. Want to come?"

"I can't not yet. I just have to sit and look beautiful," she was teasing him.

"Okay," he scooped her up and walked to the bathroom and sat her on the throne. "Now look pretty, "she did until he disrobed and her eyes got bigger and bigger. She started squirming and unbuttoning her blouse. He kept washing himself very slowly, and now her breast were hardening as he rubbed himself. "Don't do that. That's my job and she was out of her jeans, and the freckles on her breast were no longer connecting the dots. She walked to the shower, and into his arms. "It's going to be messy!"

"We are in the shower, love. It will wash away! One month of longing, but if you want to wait?" He was ready and she swooned. "Are you kidding," and she whispered, "I want...

triplets remember."

He hesitated and she was around him and he said, "Here they come ... hold on tight!"

"That was good ... but it will be better on the bench," and he agreed just so he could do it again! They ended on the floor the third time ... "Heavens I am thankful for the housekeeper and the nanny, they have given me my sexy wife back. Oh my ... you are killing me! Don't ever stop what you are doing to me," he mumbled.

They were dressed and feeding the babies in thirty minutes. Who would have thought? They were the animals that had torn that bathroom to heck. The housekeeper was speaking in Spanish very loudly.

Roscoe kissed his wife's hand and said loudly, "I speak SPANISH, but you will have much pesos in your paycheck this month and a week off!" His eyes never left Beatrice's eyes.

The housekeeper was jumping for joy as the happy couple smiled. Not one ray of embarrassment was in their eyes, for the night was not over, and they had just begun to tear things up.

Debbie came running into the library looking for Tate and the librarian was shushing her. She nodded and tiptoed to his table. She laid her evaluation of her today's dish and presentation on the table. He picked it up and it had A++. He hollered looking at the librarian, "Sorry!" and he took it to her and showed the grade to her. She jumped up and down without a word. They were all rooting for this couple.

"Let's go home! We have Guy's bike since Roscoe took the night off to be with Beatrice. "Is there somewhere special you want to go or something special you want to do to celebrate?"

"Anywhere with you is special!" One of her attackers's mother was in the library, she sneered at them and as they were going to get on the bike. The crazy woman tried to run them down. Tate called Inscoe on the phone and he was there in seconds because the security building was only two blocks away. Debbie was shaking and they got in the back seat, and called to tell Guy what had happened. Inscoe drove the bike to the security building, and locked it up and walked back. He took the kids home.

"It is a shame people like that don't teach their kids how to behave, but from the looks of it this parent never learned to behave herself. Do you want to press charges? She tried to run you over, that means attempted murder."

Debbie said, "NO! NO! I just want to go home."

Tate hugged her and nodded to Sgt. Inscoe.

Madeline and Trevor, Bruce and Jana met them at the door when they saw a security car pull up front.

They got hugs and Debbie was in that pretrial stone-faced appearance. Tate knew she was having flashbacks, and so did the others. She went straight to her room. Tate filled them in and told them about her grade and how proud she was. Then how bad it was, they almost got KILLED. He went on to their room and he held her till morning. She had not wanted to talk.

He woke once and she was sobbing.

"I love my life here. I don't want to go back."

"You are not going to let one crazy woman keep you from your dream. When you become a famous chef, you will look back on this as one day out of 365 days of this year. I will walk you to every class, and you can sit with me at the library, and Roscoe will bring us home. That is a safe plan. What do you think?"

"I will think about it," she kissed him because he was trying so hard.

They were surrounded by the most wonderful people she thought. "Tate if this had happened before I came to live here. I know, I would be with Coraine. I could not handle it without you," a tear fell. Coraine was her friend. Now she is buried.

He wiped the tears away, "You will never be alone again."

"Get some sleep or I will show you how much I love you," he said.

"I need you tonight badly," and he showed her.

She and he were so calm the next morning. All they could do, was smile.

CHAPTER SIX

Corey and Ellen came to see Tate and Debbie. They heard at the library what had happened. Ellen hugged Debbie and they went walking with the dogs at their heels. Debbie sat and rubbed Blackie's head, and Ellen sat rubbing Black Magic.

"I just love these dogs and I feel so safe when I am with them," Debbie said.

"That's good. It makes me feel better that you feel safe here," Ellen said.

"I worry about Corey. He has a fit, if someone looks at me wrong. People know he is kin to Tate. Do you think this woman is mean enough to hurt others?" Ellen was just talking and rambling, but giving Debbie more to worry about.

Debbie told her to have Corey talk to Tate about it.

That was exactly what Corey was doing. He said, "Some-one tried to run him off the road, but until now I didn't give it another thought because people have always hated skateboarders on the road." He had a motorbike now, and he was so proud of it.

"You'd think it was a Cadillac! Don't get me wrong I love it, too! We don't actually have to walk anymore," Ellen told Debbie as they walked to meet the boys.

"We don't have a vehicle at all with both of us going to college, we have to hitch a ride!" She laughed and Ellen was glad she could make her laugh. "I love it here. I love the people in this family, but the rest of the town I wouldn't give you two cents for."

"Me either! Always gossiping and my mom believes every word she hears about me and half of it is made up. MY dad use to say believe nothing you hear and only half of what you see. I miss him. He died five years ago."

"I'm sorry. Yeah, someone tells someone something, and then another tells, each adds something that is not so to it! By the time it gets back to you, you have no idea who they are talking about. I asked one person, did I really do that? You have got to be kidding! I was at home, but people saw me. NOT!" she laughed.

"Tate and I are going everywhere together. Never alone.

I advise you and Corey to go everywhere together and never go alone," Debbie said.

She promised and they were riding away on his new bike.

Corey stopped at the stoplight and Ellen had her hands in his coat pockets. She was rubbing him good.

"Do you want me to get arrested?" Corey asked.

"No ...why?" She was playing innocent.

The light was long and he said, "I cannot bring myself to take you to the woods. Anything can happen out there," he said.

"I know soon we will be eighteen and can get married. Till then we will suffer, "she made an awful face.

"Nite!" He kissed her and ran jumped on the bike. Adriana was doubled over in the bathroom, her water had broke, and she had thrown a towel down, so Unitus would not slip. She called her doctor and then she woke Unitus.

He was a wild man, he dressed in lightning speed and ran to the van cranked it up, and was driving a few feet when he realized Adriana was standing on the porch. She was so glad, he remember her and her suitcase. She was thankful it was sunrise and that he could see the road well. Then he stopped.

"What on earth are you doing?" she asked.

"I forgot to pee" and he kissed her through the window as he relieved himself. "Now that is better. I'm going to live!"

"And I'm going to have a baby ... we are going to have a baby before tomorrow!" Adriana yelled.

"What are you talking about ... she will arrive when we get to the hospital ... should I speed?" Adriana grabbed his hand and about squeezed his thumb off as a contraction hit her.

"Time it, honey! If you want to!" Her face was all distorted.

The light changed and he sped off and a blue light followed.

"Help officer! We need to get to the hospital quick ... She is having a baby!" he looked in at Adriana who was sitting still prim and proper.

"You got time ... let me write you a ticket." Then a pain hit her and she was screaming loud enough to wake up the dead .... "Can you hold her hand for a minute, officer?"

"Sure," he said. Adriana grabbed his hand and bent it backwards as the pain got worse.

She looked at him and asked, "Do you know who I am?"

"Yes ma'am, you are the lady that just BROKE my hand."

Unitus was standing back and letting Adriana take this man apart. "You had better get me to that hospital PDQ or your job is mine. I am the DA from HELL!" she screamed.

He ran and got in the police car and turned on his lights and Unitus scrambled to catch up with him.

"Good Job Honey! Now how is my honey feeling?" He slammed on brakes at the ER to keep from hitting the police car and she bumped her head on the windshield.

"Dang I forgot to belt you up ... Sorry!"

He went around and picked her up and walked her into the emergency. "Where is the delivery room? This woman is about to pop...."

The police officer said, "Take this woman back there!" pointing way away from him. The nurse got a wheelchair.

"What is that thing for? I will take my baby back there myself!" Unitus shouted.

Adriana had her cell phone in her hand and said, "Doctor come to the emergency room, if you value your life," and she screamed with pain, and the doors opened, and the magical doctor had all of them flying in every direction to help her!

One of the executives of the hospital had been summoned to greet Marcus the Billionaire's daughter. He wanted that wing for his hospital ... really bad.

"Whatever you need just let me know!" he said.

"I need this baby to come OUT! ... Can you help me?" The man in the business suit fainted.

"Adriana honey ... now look what you have done darling! Can you ease up on the right shoulder? Oh what the heck! Go for it, honey … rip it apart. They'll sew it up, Sweetums." They were in a room. She completely stripped with one motion. He put the sheet up to cover her.

The nurse asked if she wanted a gown and Adriana growled at her, and showed some teeth.

"Now now honey! You may need some of these kind people before the night is up!" he gulped.

"OH shut up! and get me that sorry ass Dr. Silverstein that is getting paid to do NOTHING!" She was having another contraction … a big one.

"Honey, he is scared to come in here. He is afraid you might break his hand like you did that nice young policeman. They are putting it in a cast as we speak," Unitus stated.

"Unitus love, do you want to see your baby? Then get someone in here quick to give me some drugs before I reach down and pull her out … MYSELF!"

"Yes dear!" He went to Silverstein and lifted him high in the air, "She says if you don't deliver that baby now, she is going to pull her out. Please doc! Don't let her hurt my baby girl. Please!" and he sat him down and walked back in with Adriana. "He said he would be right here! And look here he is!".... ANGEL RENEE POMMEL was born thirty minutes later … 7lbs 12oz. No drugs were needed. There was no time. The most beautiful little girl Unitus had ever seen lie on her mother's belly as he cut the cord. Adriana was cooing at the baby and completely calm … a civilized woman … a vision of feminine beauty.

The complete opposite of the deranged person that was screaming .... "kill that doctor"... thirty minutes ago.

Unitus kissed his wife and said, "You did good, Mama!"

Adriana looked at Unitus for the first time. He was cut and bruised and had bite marks on him. His clothes were torn half off and he was smiling at her.

She said, "Did I do that?"

He shook his head up and down still smiling and blew her an air kiss. No way was he going to get close to her again this day.

The nurse swaddled the baby after footprints and weight were done. She handed "Angel" to him, Adriana was crying softly. "She is sooo beautiful can someone take a picture of her and him with his phone."

"I want a picture of my wife with the baby first."

None of the staff was going to tell this crazy woman that she could not take pictures in this room.

As Unitus left to park the van, he passed the police officer and told him he was very sorry and thanked him for getting them here.

He said, "You'll be getting my bill sir, but no ticket from me. You deserve a medal!"

He passed the administrator and asked him how his head was and he said, "Just fine. You look like a war casualty."

"My victory day!" His leg hurt, he saluted on his way out.

CHAPTER SEVEN

The hospital was abuzz about the DA and the War Hero. The news caption: OFFICER & A GENTLEMAN have their first baby and a new hospital wing will be built and named after the baby, the Angel Renee Pommel Building. The song by Jennifer Warren and Joe Crocker was playing, "Up where the eagles fly on a mountain high," Adriana and Unitus were so proud.

Unitus told Bruce, "Thank God there were no video camera recording of my wife!" Bruce said, "Oh there was plenty and Marcus is negotiating to have the hospital's security camera footage destroyed. Why do you think he had the wing dedicated this quick. It's to mask your wife's criminal behavior on that footage," and he laughed.

"Shut your face, Bruce. YOU told them I was a war hero … didn't you? I can't believe you did that!" Unitus was so mad and dangerously quiet.

Bruce had to backpedal. "Unitus she broke a man's hand. She threaten most every staff member with their life. She threatened to have the doctor KILLED. You, my friend are on the camera picking up a doctor my the collar, and walking him into Adriana's ER room. Now ask me again, why I painted you as a sweet loveable war hero. Now next time you are on the camera, PULL that pant leg up a little so the public will believe my story! I saved your ass this time and Adriana's father saved hers. Just say thank you!" Bruce smiled widely.

Unitus said simply, "Thank You."

They went to the nursery and there stood Marcus Buchanan holding the baby in a surgical gown and inside the nursery. He was holding the little "Angel" and rocking her in his arms.

Unitus said, "I got to get a picture of this," and he pulled his phone out and snapped several for Adriana and for her father.

"Come on Bruce, let's get a selfie with them in the background. Unitus turned his head and said, "Say cheeseeeeee grandpa!"

He took it to Adriana to see. She was asleep with the TV still blasting the "Breaking News: Billionaire Marcus Buchanan's donation was over Seven Million Dollars. What a day for our hospital and the entire wing will be for Pediatric Care of Sick Children."

Adriana was opening her eyes and there Unitus stood in his business suit that her father liked. He showed her, her father inside the nursery with Angel. She started crying. "I never knew how much he cared until now. Unitus darn it, I guess we are going to have to go see him in Dallas."

In walks her father and he says, "Why in the world would you guys want to go all that way to Dallas to see me?"

Adriana looked at Unitus and he shrugged his shoulders.

"For heaven's sakes. I bought a house over the hill and through the woods. Well actually it hasn't been built yet, but it will be. In the next three to six months, I am hopefully going to enjoy my daughter and her family. The only family that doesn't ask me for the moon. That Angel is going to know who her grandfather really is, not just a picture on the wall.

You know Adriana, I spent my whole life building businesses, now I want to sit back, out of the rat race, and enjoy."

"Daddy you deserve to enjoy. You have worked so hard. Thank you for all that you have done in Angel's namesake. Unitus and I will be forever grateful."

"Adriana you did not tell me Unitus was a war hero!"

"He's not a bragger Daddy, that's why I love him and because he has big muscles and …."

Unitus ahem, "That's enough honey!" He was pulling at his pant's leg and looking at Bruce.

Bruce was shaking his head so he sat down. He never let his artificial leg shine, but there was a reason today.

He was in training and he wanted some of his military buddies to be able to train with him, but they needed sponsors. Maybe it was a bad idea today, Bruce was right.

With the news team here though, the viewers were always funding somebody. The help did not have to come from Mr. Moneybags over there.

He had to keep up his training even with a newborn, so it was going to be a challenge.

More challenging in six months was going to be dealing with his father- in -law living down the road. Mercy!

Spot on … the interviewer caught sight of his leg, "Sir did you lose your leg in the war?"

Unitus frowned and said, "Yes, a grenade took it, but I don't let it get me down. I want any vets to come join me in training for the triathlon held in ….. We need funds for our vets to compete. Would you Mr. Commentator have a website that anyone could give to help my buddies get funded?"

"Why yes, we will set one up and name it the ANGEL POMMEL FUND for DISABLED VETS! Anyone can help this worthy cause at our TV website," he said.

The interviewer afterward was shaking Unitus's hand and he was elated to have made National news. He was grinning into the camera and talking it up. This man with this one interview was advancing his own career, and he owed it all to Unitus. He promised to continue documenting the cause, if Unitus gave him permission to video his training, etc. Unitus agreed which shocked Adriana.

Adriana winked at Unitus, "You did good, Honey! Our daughter isn't 24 hours old and she has made local and national news and benefited so many. Not one but two projects with her name on them. Can you believe it!"

"Quite frankly, NO!" he was kissing her and looked around to a flashbulb. "Okay fellows that's a wrap!" pointing to the door for them to leave.

Marcus came and patted him on the back, "You did good, son. I am proud of the way you handled yourself. Adriana you didn't tell me about his leg?" he had said it again.

"It doesn't DEFINE him, daddy. I want you to love him for himself like I do!" she was gushing at Unitus and Marcus could see he had competition for his daughter's heart. For once, it was OK to be second. Strange, but OK. This one time.

Madeline and Trevor met Marcus at THE INN restaurant for supper. Of course, she had to dress for the occasion. Trevor was not happy with his getup either, so he loosened the tie.

"Hello! Hello! My dear friends!" Marcus was beaming, "Have you seen her? The granddaughter." Marcus was shaking hands and people even in the restaurant were taking photos of him. He was use to it, but they were not.

"Yes on the news and Unitus text us with an attachment. She is beautiful just like her mother," Madeline stated because it was the truth.

"How about that son-in-law of yours, ain't he something?"

Trevor always knew something horrific had taken Unitus's leg, but he hadn't known the circumstances till today when the news reported it."

"Yes, Adriana did good. She picked out a winner, not the sleazes I kept sending her way. I like to call them the test factors. We tested them and the facts proved what kind of men, they truly were. Have you seen my spitfire of a daughter in a courtroom, she can pick a man apart. Same in her dating, I have been privileged to watch it through the years. I never thought she would settle down." Marcus was wound up and ordered a bourbon and coke.

"Sorry folks, how was your day?" Marcus was so use to being the center of attention, he forgot to let others speak. He was going to have to practice and be more mindful of what he said. This town moves at a snail's pace.

"We rode our trike and I cooked everyone breakfast this morning. That's about it!" Madeline smiled into Trevor's eyes.

Marcus nodded for Trevor to speak, "Oh I took the horse out for a spin and ran the dogs. That's about it," he grinned at Madeline. Neither he nor Madeline was going to detail what else they did this morning. He laughed.

Marcus said, "What's so funny? Finally the meal is here!"

They started eating their entree and Marcus stated, "This is delicious. Good old southern cooking. I do enjoy this and I think I could get use to it."

Madeline eyed Marcus, "And what might you have up your sleeve? I depict the sound that you like it here."

"You always zero right in, don't you? Don't answer that. You and Trevor have been my friends for approximately little over thirty years!" he sat back and stretched as he sipped his piping hot coffee.

"Can't get anything pass you two. I have a house near yours. Planned it that way." Madeline was looking at Trevor and smiling. They both knew what that meant.

Trevor sipped his usual brandy and sternly looked at Marcus, "You cannot come and build here. We are peaceful here. NO, Marcus. NO! We don't want you here, if you bring your baggage."

"I see you don't think this hick town needs a highrise hotel and casino? Hmm," Marcus laced his fingers and propped on the table.

"Madeline what do you think?" Marcus queried.

"I like it just like it is. We built our home like the one in Dallas here. Never would we want Hendersonville in Dallas. The two do not mix, Marcus. Don't come and destroy your grandchild's privacy. Let her grow up with nature and no concrete sidewalks," she placed her napkin in her plate. She was done.

Trevor said, "Well put my dear!" and he patted her hand.

"I see your point. I have to turn off my business mind while I am here. There is great potential here. C 'est la vie! I will forget it for now! I know you are happy here. Maybe I will be also. There is that grain of salt that I hope I find the same happiness here as you two. Thank you for being honest with me!"

"We have always been and will always be, my friend." Trevor shook his hand and they walked out together.

"Where are you staying? Can we offer you lodging while you are here?"

"Thank you maybe next time. I have a cab coming to take me to the airport in Charlotte and I'll be back in Dallas by 4:00pm for a meeting. Take care of my loved ones," he kissed Madeline on the her slender hand and gave Trevor a bear hug that Trevor had to bend down to get.

The cab was there and they waved him goodbye.

"He is a wheeler-dealer! Lord knows ... he is going to reek havoc ... if he comes in here and tries to change anything."

"He said he wouldn't Trev," Madeline stated.

"Do you REALLY believe that?" Trevor shook his head.

PART TWELVE

CHAPTER ONE

The warden had Chris brought from solitary in to talk to him. His eyes were not able to focus yet due to the sunshine flooding the office.

"Sit down and let us discuss something of importance to both of us. I have brought you here to hire you to bomb my cousin's car. I don't want his family hurt. I want them to suffer like he made my family. He will never see it coming. You see, he trusts me. That is why he moved you here to me so I would keep you here."

"I like that. I love nothing better than blowing people up. What is your plan Mr Porter, or should I say Mr. Warden?"

"I will let you out by accident, and you go do your job. I know you have accomplices. So you can round them up, take your time and do it by July 4th my Independence Day!"

"That's a four month span ... man ... how do I evade capture Oh mighty one?" sarcastic Chris came forward with his questions.

"That is for you ... to figure out ... not me," he chuckled.

Chris grinned, "I shall have a piece of ass before this day is through!"

"Did I say you were leaving today? You so much as lay a finger on a real woman, I will kill you myself. You WILL be captured, and I will burn you at the stake. Is that clear?"

"Crystal clear ... Oh mighty one!" he grinned that toothless grin. He had heard the warden liked him some young virgins and he raped them in the prison. What a crock! He just doesn't want to share, the self righteous bastard.

"Can I have your leftovers sir?" He grinned. "Yea, you have a squealing pig here, he told me all. When I get out, I will let you have MY virgin leftovers."

Warden Porter was gritting his teeth and his nostrils were flaring, just the mention of a virgin made him hard, and this convict knew it. He took his whip and struck the table, but he did not hit Chris who did not flinch. Chris just grinned.

"So be it! When the job is done, you can have them!" The warden knew he would have Chris shot on return to his prison. No better than that, he himself will shoot him between the eyes. He will never touch one of his pretties. He rubbed his crotch to validate its desire for only the purest.

On the way back to solitary, he nodded at a guard and that let him know it was a deal brewing. He had to have an inside prison working system, if the warden was stupid enough to let him back out into the open facility.

He tripped so he could tie his shoe while looking for his contact Joe. There he was pushing a laundry cart. He nodded. The innocent guard walked his prisoner to his cell where Chris knocked him in the head, and put him into his bed.

Wrapped him up under his blanket and tucked him in the position that he usually slept.

With this uniform on, he found the laundry cart guy, and they went around the corner. Chris was inside the cart and being pushed to the van with tools. He climbed in and sat until the man got in, and he provided a duffel bag with his company logo on it, and the clothes fit even the shoes.

"Don't move for any reason just scribble on the notebook as if you are calculating the job measures. He put him in front as a passenger because they checked the van thoroughly.

The guy had left the officers clothes by the trash can. They always checked the trashcans.

He was out and the man said, "I will drop you off at the job and you can change, and we will go to my car and drive away as normal.

"You can pay now or your boss can pay me later. Jung must be one hell of a friend to you. He's paying one million. No way I would do it for less, Good day!"

"I am worth every dime ... now buzz off!" Jung's men whisked Chris off to the smugglers hideaway south of Dallas.

"Evening ... tea or bong?" Jung asked.

"A beer and a prostitute in that order!" Jung clapped his hands and it was done.

The next day Chris stretched. He was clean, shaven, hair cut, and the woman that had bathed him sure did know, what a man liked. "Damn forgot to ask her name ...."

Adriana and Unitus were still staring at their bundle of joy who was sleeping in her mother's arms after nursing.

"She's a lucky little girl to have ...." He ran a finger around her areola and her vagina contracted, and he saw her tightening. He finished the sentence, "the most perfect bottles I have ever seen ... makes me want to suck the milk right out of them..." and he did.

She grabbed her stomach and made a face as if in pain.

"What what's wrong … Honey! Honey speak to me!" Unitus was whispering not to wake up the baby.

"Come closer," she put her tongue in his ear and licked it but good. She smiled and bit his lip while holding the baby close.

"Oh you have started something and you are going to finish it!" he said.

"But the baby?" she purred. "Really?" he said staring at her.

"She has been for eight and half months rocked every night so she I'd say … is pretty use to us by now," he smiled.

"Let's go in the bathroom now," he was doubled over.

"No, not with the baby wait till they pick her up" she cooed.

"Okay and when will that be?" he asked.

"An hour or two!" she teased.

"You are kidding?" he was pouting and she licked his lips.

She laughed, "No when I push that little red button."

He started pushing it and pushing it.

"Stop that's for emergencies,"

"This is an emergency!" She bopped him on his head.

"May I help you?" the intercom asked.

"The baby is sleeping. Can someone put her in her crib?"

"Of course. I'll send someone right in …" click and the red light was off.

A nurse from the nursery came and took the baby as he was still rubbing his temple.

"Now come here darling!" She had on the black short negligee that Jana brought her and she started to get up.

He said, "Stop where you are! Don't get up! These people have seen enough of my wife's private parts!"

"What are you talking about?" she glared at him.

"You must have knocked some sense into me. They have cameras everywhere ... in the rooms, in the ER, in the delivery room and even in the parking lots..." She was holding her mouth ... she was having flashbacks of her pre-delivery behavior ... "OH MY GOD!"

Patting her and saying, "Breath honey! Breath!" she gasp and took a breath.

"What am I going to do?" she said softly.

He had tortured her enough, "Nothing darling. Daddy Moneybags bought a wing in exchange for those tapes and he and I burned them. That's how close we are!" he took his index and first finger and squeezed them together referring to his new relationship with his father-in-law.

She said, "Thank you," quietly she was looking around.

"I just don't want them to get a Pamela and Tommy Lee tape floating around here ... do you?" Unitus grinned.

She was shaking her head non-stop, "No dear! You are right!"

"We could go to the van?" he smiled.

"Parking lots have cameras?" she repeated.

He snapped his fingers, "Dang. I did say that. Didn't I ... I see your wheels turning and I know my baby ... if there's a will. There's a way!"

"There's one of Roscoe's guards on every floor and one on this floor. Right?" she said.

Then we walk to this one, and you tell them to guard the door ... NO ONE ALLOWED... same for the roof guy, Voila!"

"I will go check for cameras in the stairwell," he said.

"NO! We will check ... I don't trust you with the affairs of the heart. You will say anything to get in my panties!"

"Now we're talking! Sit down! You've done it again!"

"Put a towel over your arm. Do I have to think of everything?" she said.

"No problem. You killed it with your mouth! There it's back again. Just the mention of your mouth."

"Let's go before you wear that yo-yo out!" she put her robe on very very slowly, and boing!

"You are a sadist!" he tied the knot to her robe. "Now walk close to me and smile up adoringly at me."

They walked the walk until they saw the guard, and he agreed to hold the door. Once in, he was looking for a camera, there was none and the guard above agreed to hold that door.

"What I do for the love of your..." she swallowed his tongue.

He breathed deeply. She pulled him in. He was lost.

"Tomorrow a team will search for a dead body here. My blood type will match! Still there's no pictures! Yay"

Unitus was running using his blade leg and he had adjusted his bike to use the blade for pedaling. It had been trial and error, and he didn't use either for the swimming distance, and that he had to figure out. He had no problem at home in their pool, off and dive in, but on a beach he would have to have both legs to run to the deep and from the deep ocean. This blade was too heavy, but would a thinner one break when running or cycling? He would talk to the experts. Maybe they had a company who would want him to test it. Otherwise, he had to invest in a lighter one and that meant money. So he would train hard as he is doing until he could swing it.

Exhaustion was getting to be the daily routine. Even Adriana said, "Honey you got to slow down."

"Never did I think I would hear you say that, but I will some when you come home," and he smiled.

"There's my Angel," he took the baby to the window and showed her the moon and stars.

"Are you coming home tomorrow?" he asked as he swung Angel from side to side.

"Yes whenever my husband can find time to come and get us," Adriana said as if she was being ignored.

"Okay you hold her," he put her in her arms. Then he picked both of them up, and he was swinging them from side to side when the doctor walked in.

Adriana was smiling from ear to ear.

Dr. Silverstein said, "I see our little mother is a very happy woman. I see a father with a future herniated disc."

"Just kidding. I have written discharge orders for tomorrow morning unless you can think of anything preventing it.

"All systems go, Doc! Let's get the show on the road."

"Unitus, Honey! He didn't say tonight!"

"I hate sleeping without you!" he admitted.

"You can have her one more night after that she is mine!"

He shook the doctor's hand.

"Bruce ask Debbie, if she can help Adriana, if she needs it so I can train. I am bringing them home tomorrow or ask Jana if she can help!" Unitus was in panic mode talking to Bruce.

"You are lost … at a lost of what to do and that is normal, Bro. Now sit down and take a deep breath. Talk to me …"

"I haven't a clue what to do. Madeline maybe she would be a better choice to help. That's an experienced woman. Can I talk to her? I need a back up plan for tomorrow."

Madeline said into the phone that she would be there for him. Debbie said she didn't know a thing as did Jana.

"I will call Kyleigh and Beatrice for you, son. That's what family is for, if not to help out. You just ask anytime. K & B know-it-all about babies! So you get a good night's sleep and we will support you in all you do. Love you! Nite!" Madeline hung up and turned to Trevor.

"You'd better give that boy one of your nerve pills!" she said.

"Yes, dear. Let's get some shut-eye! Goodnight, Mary Ellen!" Trevor said.

"Goodnight, John Boy!" she sighed. He did that when he was tired and didn't want to be bothered.

CHAPTER TWO

Cain and Caleb came running into the nursery to see their new sisters BeBe and FiFi. Roscoe was right behind them.

"You boys, got to be careful. Don't touch. Just kiss. Okay?"

"Okay, daddy!" high - fived Cain and Caleb did the same.

They were identicals but their voices were so different. So Roscoe had no problem ID'ing them and their manners were really kicking in. That stern taskmaster of a nanny was paying off.

The girls were in Beatrice's arms dressed in pink onesies. After the kisses, the nanny took the boys to the yard to play and to run some energy off.

Roscoe took FiFi and sat in the rocker beside Beatrice and BeBe. "Honey, do you have to go to work? I miss you so much ..."

Beatrice was up to something Roscoe was frowning and then FiFi was frowning. He was so excited, "Did you see that Beatrice? She was doing the trademark Roscoe!" Beatrice said, "Honey, be for real! She is pooping in her diaper!"

"Oops time for work! Gotta go!" and gave FiFi to Beatrice.

He was going to feel of her gorgeous ... "Kiss, but don't touch!" same as he had told the boys.

"We'll talk tonight. Love you!" and he was gone.

"You girls must learn this early in life. If there is shit to clean up, the men start running! Whether you are two weeks old or twenty two years old, but mama will teach you a trick!"

"This is called an intercom, darlings ... and when you marry into a wealthy family all you have to do is press a button, and shit is gone! Voila!" They were smiling and farting and Beatrice was laughing.

She would wait until they were good and finished. Then she would press the button, and either the housekeeper or the nanny would wash her babies. While she would sigh and go back to bed. To fake a feeble walk was working every time, next week she would miraculously recover.

Kyleigh was coming over and they were going to write a list for poor Unitus. He and Adriana knew nothing about babies.

"Zilch Zero Nada!" Kyleigh said.

"So they need a nanny, an old woman like you picked out for me. I really think Adriana would go for that. They are both professional people. Did you know Unitus was in the CIA?"

"Me neither. A graduate of Harvard. I thought he graduated from Harley-Davidson, the first time I met him."

They both laughed and then got serious. "Either way, we love them. Right?"

"Kyleigh can go with Madeline! Be sure and tell Adriana that I would bring my four, but she would no longer be living on the mountain. They would have it pulled down by noon," Beatrice rued.

"I think I will go shopping today Kyleigh," Beatrice looked at her friend.

"Of course, online?" Kyleigh grinned. "I'll be back."

Jung told Chris Shackleford that BRUCE SMITH was his target. "This is the man ... you blow up. He interfered with the wrong person!" He took a hit from his opium bong and inhaled deeply. "When he shutdown my smuggling operation, we were friends, then I learned he was undercover CIA...."

His laugh was hideous, and his slanted eyes were glassy, and Chris saw the evil and the depth of this man.

"You have the same hate, I have for the Smiths ... Have no fear once I do an operation of this magnitude ... Bombs bursting in air.... all to smithereens!" hehee hehee "We are a good team Jung, but I'll never turn my back on you!"

"Nor I you! Now leave I'll pay you when I see the obituary!"

Jung had given him money to buy lodgings and he supplied all the materials for the explosives that he would need.

In the meantime Warden Porter had called Trevor.

"Poor cuz! We had a BREAKOUT. Yes, he is on the loose! I have every law officer in this state looking for him. It was well planned. He had someone on the outside that planned it expertly. I am so sorry! I will contact you if we apprehend him, and you do the same. Later."

Trevor was in shock. "Two states away and he is on his way here to kill all the Smiths he can." He was talking to Roscoe, and Guy via Skype. They were all in shock.

"We may can get Adam out and he can find him. He has the street contacts and knows Chris like a book. He loves Tate and will do ANYTHING for him, and not for us. Chris forced Adam to do the elevator thing, and used Tate as the bargaining chip. Chris did not have any feelings for either boy. That is one option," Trevor said.

"My Army, Marine and Seabees ... brothers can do the hunting also and take him out, but it will take some time for that. That is option two."

"Guy do you have any suggestions?" "I know the witness protection can offer us a refuge. Trevor ... Kyleigh will never ever return to me as she is now. She is doing so well. I have to get her as far away from here, as I can and fast. Forgive me, I am a little crazy right now!"

"That is understandable. You do what you got to do!"

"Roscoe, any suggestions?"

"I am thinking about how perfect this day began and now POW, the bubble has been burst. I have Beatrice and the kids to think about, PLUS her mother and father will be devastated after what they have been through. I am with Guy, we need to get as far away from here as we possible can get quickly!"

"So you two are saying run and leave the rest of the family to perish. Hmm! I have your grandma to think of, and the teenagers that have been through HELL this year, and Bruce and Jana... Oh my God I have to get to Unitus and Bruce. Maybe they will have some different ideas! I'll touch base later. Love you two boys!"

Trevor got Unitus on Skype prior to leaving the hospital and he had called Bruce and Jana. Madeline marched in and sat down ... might as well get Tate and Debbie in here too!

Madeline phoned them to come. She was not going to leave this room. They came running.

"We have a family crisis. Chris Shackleford has escaped and is on his way to kill this family. MY cousin said the breakout was well-planned, a professional job. So someone wants us enough to risk anything to have this explosive expert annihilate us! I have talked to Roscoe and Guy and got their suggestions. Now Bruce you and Unitus, can put your heads together and get back with me on your suggestions."

"Unitus my best to you and Adriana and the baby. Sorry I had to spring this on you before she comes home. You can bring her here if you want! He broke out two states away depending on who is helping him will mean how long it will take for him to get here. We will be ready!"

Madeline asked, "Does Kyleigh know?"

"Yes I have talked to both the boys," Trevor was a listener but no one was talking.

He shared with Tate what was one of the plans. "He will do it for me and a chance to freedom … would … could he get his sentence gone, if he finds and kills Chris. That is something that he would fight for … I know he hates Chris for what he has put us through Trevor?"

"WE will talk about it! I am all for having someone inside his system of thieves and cutthroats, and we have our team backing them! That way we have two teams at work on the same page with one goal in mind."

"Madeline do you have any ideas?"

"You have forgotten about Lefty and my merry maids that know everything that's happening in this town," she said.

Unitus arrived at the hospital in a glum mood, it should have been a happy day.

He had to fill Adriana in and he sat her down and he began the story, "I want you and Angel to get on a plane today and stay with your father till this is done."

"I will not leave you my husband, the father of my child and the love of my life. I WILL call Daddy Moneybags and ask him to send an army to protect us and all our family here," she smiled and was not afraid at all.

"I am not letting a lunatic deprave my baby of her nursery. The nursery she is to grow into, and her crib will turn into a twin bed, and as a teenager she will redecorate her room into a cool pad for her friends to visit her on her mountaintop. No we will not run. This is our home. I love you, but my place is with you! Understood! So don't ask again!" she stared at him.

"You have an air about you when you are trying a case and talking to the jury to sway their opinion to your way of thinking, and I agree we will not run. Call your father before we leave, so I will have peace in my heart and don't do that again!'

"What?" she stared at him.

"Walk in front of me, strutting like a peacock, and jiggling, and wetting your lips... as you talk pure poetry to my ears. I am so in love with you ... I could pop!' and he grabbed her before the baby was brought in, because the way this morning was going, he may not have another chance.

"Every minute is precious. None are promised, and I don't want to waste a one!" Unitus said.

"Me either prosecutor. You know you would make a GOOD lawyer, husband of mine, and leave your training for our eyes only! I still have a lot to train you in!" he was getting ....

"What? There can't be anything we haven't tried. Is there?" he questioned her.

She fluffed her hair and flipped it over one shoulder and said, "There's changing diapers, burping, helping me pump my breast milk into a bottle that you can hold and feed the baby, and the list goes on." She smiled and whispered in his ear what he was going to learn tonight in their bedroom.

"Okay where is your coat I have to throw it over my arm again?" Unitus grimaced.

"Is my honey complaining again. Let me see if I can't make it better." She sat on his lap and wiggled.

They brought the baby in and she did not move to get her so they brought her to Adriana. The nurse said she would be right back.

"Adriana honey! What is wrong?" She was not crying, she was laughing.

"My lacy undies are caught on your massive zipper. Can you slide my panties off, then I can save the lace."

"Okay, Maybe not okay…Okay Maybe not okay! This is not going well!" Unitus could not take them off with the baby in her lap. If he took them off only one thing was going to happen for sure.

Adriana turned her head and stretched her neck as Angel was suckle her breast. "You know what happens when you suck my breasts" she was tighten and relaxing … he could feel it.

"Oh God No.. Stop before I rip them off!"

"Rip them! Rip them! The way the day is going, we may not have another chance."

He ripped them and the baby burped, "Good Job, darling!"

"I was talking to the baby, Yes we Yes we oh baby!" the nurse walked in oblivious of what was happening and she was reading her discharge papers.

While the daddy is taking a nap. His eyes are closed and he is snoring loudly while his wife is feeding the baby with her legs wide open. What a strange family the student nurse thought, not for me to judge. She went on her merry way and said, "Transportation will be by in a few or in the next hour."

Adriana stuttered," O O Okay!" and smiled. Angel was now asleep and she had no panties on, and her husband was so relaxed. He was about to recline in the chair and ask for more.

"No! We have to go home or do you want to stay here?"

Needing to do some repair work, he went to her bathroom and locked the door. She washed at the sink and she hear the shower running. "Dang what a man? Get your money's worth honey!"

"Don't pack that hair dryer! I'm going to need it. I had to wash my pants and I can get them dry in ten minutes," Unitus shouted.

"Why do you have this door locked?" she asked.

"To protect myself from my wife!" Unitus shouted again.

She was changing the baby and cuddling her and told Angel, "Your daddy is blow drying his!"

"This is what the doc ordered. You gotta love his hospital!" Unitus came barreling out stating as fact to his beautiful wife.

Adriana had phoned her father, "Please have them all check in with Mr. Trevor when they get here. Thank you, daddy! I love you and so does Unitus and so does Angel! Yes I will call you!"

Unitus and Adriana stopped the van and went in to see Trevor and Madeline. All hugs and kisses and oohs and aahs followed and pictures were taken. So far Angel had not been put down and had not whimpered a bit!

The men had not come out of the den and they had the door locked. Adriana said, "I don't understand why men are always locking the doors inside the house. I have always lock the outside doors. Please explain?" looking at Madeline, Kyleigh, and Beatrice.

"It's a man thingy honey! Don't worry about it! We got to get you a dog today!" Madeline said.

"A dog?" Adriana asked.

"Blackie or Black Magic your choice they can break a door down! Ask Kyleigh?" GM continued.

"Yeah we have replaced one twice, but now we feel good about our dog. He has trained us!" Kyleigh was smiling this mess was not getting to her as long as everyone was around her. Madeline was going to tell Guy to bring her here, if he ever had to leave the house for any reason.

"Adriana honey when Unitus has to leave your house for any reason, have him drop you and the baby off by here!" mother-hen was gathering her brood.

"Thanks I will!" Adriana did feel safe here. She had chosen Black Magic for her dog. The trainer would be here tomorrow and thank goodness the panic button had been installed while she was in the hospital.

Everything was falling into place. It was just a matter of coordinating everything. The SBI and FBI had set up here at Trevor's.

Madeline's old house will be where Marcus's men can stay when they get here from Texas. There were no hotels and Trevor was at wits end, and said it out loud.

"I guess Marcus is right we do need ONE big highrise hotel here, but a casino no way! There is one nearby at Cherokee. I will mention it to him soon."

Unitus gave him the thumbs up, as if to say I will mention it, too!

CHAPTER THREE

"Tate told me at the library that Uncle Chris is out of prison," Corey told his mother, Eunice. "Tate will not be able to come by for fear Chris might harm us. He says it is the Smiths he wants dead, but he just wanted us to know and to call him, if we hear from him. I told him we would." "I'm glad he told you and I am so glad you are graduating next week. Your father would be so proud. Now all I have to do is get your brother through junior high. Jennifer will be home from college tomorrow. She has a spring break. She says she is bringing someone with her."

"I will be so glad to see her. I haven't wrote to her like I should have. I think she will understand when she sees my GPA for the year. She has always been the brainac in the family. Did she say whether she was bringing a boy? a girl?"

His mother gasped, "Corey do you know something I don't know? Has she said she has been dating?" Eunice asked.

"Nah! Just playing with you, Mom!" Corey like to tease her that Jennifer was going to go wild at college and run off with a guy and get married. "She wouldn't come home if she was married or pregnant."

"Boy ... shut your mouth before I do!" Eunice said as she finished her ironing.

"Sorry, Mom," he grabbed the trash bag and did his chore taking it to the curb and tossing it into the dumpster.

"Are you going to the library tonight?" she yelled from the porch.

"Yes after I leave work," Corey said.

"Okay! Have a good day, son!" Eunice said as she was going back into the house.

"Jason are you ready for school. We have got to get going! Move it, Move it, Move it," Eunice's husband use to say that to all the kids. His military motto was if you got to be some-where ... Be early. Never late!" Geez she missed him.

Jason went running past her and jumped off the porch. He was sitting in the front seat playing a Nintendo game when she got into the car.

"Did you brush your teeth?" she asked. "Come here and let me check," that was their morning ritual. He opened his mouth and she would kiss him on the cheek. He did not want her to hug or kiss him at school, now that he was in Jr-Hi.

As she drove she said to herself, this is my last one. All my children are growing up. A tear fell, soon she would be alone. Cassie her friend at church had told her that she had a man she wanted her to meet. She was a matchmaker and busybody, but she had been a true friend through the years. Their husbands had served together, and Eunice might give it a go.

"Hello Cassie. Can we meet for lunch? Burger King will be fine at 12:15. See you then, BYE." Eunice hung up and went into work. She had worked as a receptionist for Royster Martin & Royster for six years now. She loved what she did and met a lot of business people and some real folks. It was a job and it helped pay the bills since her husband's death.

Cassie met her and they had a good talk. "It's about time you went out Eunice, you are too pretty a woman to just waste away!" she was making Eunice smile a little.

"When can we go shopping, and no you cannot buy old fuddy- duddy clothes? I am picking you out something that will attract a man, not push him away," Cassie was too loud.

"Cassie lower your voice … the whole town doesn't have to know my business," Eunice looked down at her French fries, but she didn't eat them. She had put herself on a diet two months ago and she had lost 25 lbs.

"Shopping? Look at what you are wearing. That law office doesn't care what you look like, but I do. If you went to work all fancied up, they would all pass out." Cassie was laying it on thick. It was the truth. That was what she loved about Cassie, she was not two-faced like some of her so called friends. Theresa was the worst.

"Hmm when you put it that way, tomorrow around ten and I am going to open up my first clothing account just for me. I've never done that, it has always been for the kids!" She held her head up higher than usual when she walked back into the law office and smiled at everyone.

One of the girls that did the filing said, "I want the same thing she had for lunch. Darn, I have already eaten," grinning at Eunice.

Cassie had been on the phone with several of the military wives talking up what single male was available for Eunice.

The next day Eunice was so excited that Corey was taking Jason skateboarding and she hugged and kissed them till they both said, "Stop please! Stop someone might see you."

"Who?" I don't care I love my boys," and she jumped in the car with Cassie and they drove off.

Both boys were standing at the curb with their mouths open," Was that our Mom? I didn't know she could run that fast!" Jason said.

"Me neither … so I guess we had better let her kiss us again brother. You must be HIGH TEST and I'm UNLEADED," said Corey.

"If we ever become special agents and need a handle, they sound like good code names to use," Jason said. He was into comic books and action heroes on his XBOX and Nintendo.

"Sounds like you need to back off them games for awhile little High Test," Corey said.

They were veering around a curve and the car just missed Corey again. The same woman and Jason had nowhere to go, but over a trashcan and wrecked his knee.

"Don't tell Mom! She will never let me skateboard with you again," he blew on his knee as if it would help the scrape.

"It wasn't your fault. It was a crazy lady! She can't drive!" he laughed and helped Jason stand.

"Walk and shake it off. If it still hurts to walk, we got to tell mom," Corey stated.

"It's just a scrape!" and he walked and jumped. "It's OK!"

Marcus was livid when his daughter talked to him. "I will send my plane with the men and you and your family come here. I would personally wring this man's neck, if he hurt one hair, one either of your heads."

"Daddy the SBI and the FBI are staying at Mr. Trevor's and he says to tell you a high rise hotel here is much needed!"

"OH Wow! I am on my way, Baby girl. Then this is bad news with a twist of good news."

She could see her father's wheels turning through the phone. He had not been needed by anyone for a long time. This was a chance for him to make a name for himself in the township for bringing something much needed to the community, and protect his family in one swoop. As he would say, "I'm just mixing business with pleasure, honey!"

Unitus had took his family to the top, and Adriana was so relieved. Little Angel was fussy and had her first crying spell on top of the mountain when Adriana LAID HER DOWN. "I was told this would happen," talking to herself.

"It's good for her," Unitus said, "It expands her lungs and makes them healthy, or does she just want her mommy's tits like I do?" he laughed.

He grabbed her and kissed her. "She is quiet. Let's go see if everything is okay!" The monitor was a blessing. They tiptoed to the nursery and there she was looking around at the cow turning and jumping over the moon.

We can see her on the video monitor screen on the TV in the kitchen, "Let's cook, woman!" "You can't possibly be hungry again after all you ate at Trevor's?" she looked at him.

"You are right again, but that is not what I am hungry for?"

He had her in his arms.

"Do you realize … I just had a baby?" Adriana was patting her foot.

He shook his head "Yes, dear! Are you saying you have your first headache since we have been married? I truly understand my little pumpkin," as he was nuzzling her neck and unzipping her skirt and she was unzipping his pants and making hickeys everywhere.

"OH I am aching, but it is not cranial pain that I have, oh husband of mine. There's just one thing that I want to make very clear and you must promise me," she was licking at his navel.

"OH God I have missed you! ANYTHING I promise!" She stood and looked him into his eyes.

"That you will clean this mess up when we are through because I have to clean the baby when she wakes," he was thinking and she was waiting.

He was rubbing her buttocks and thinking, "NO problem!" He picked her up and she fought him.

"Not like that," she straddled him and eased down. "Now that is more like it." She sucked on his tongue till they got to the bed.

"Now that's more like it," and they tumbled into bed.

"I have missed you so much. Didn't sleep at all in this bed. Slept in the recliner. Could not without you!" they made love.

Eunice and Cassie went shopping, "I've got to have some-thing to wear for Corey's graduation and something to wear on a blind date. Definitely something more up-to-date for the office, too" They went to customer service to get her card and demanded "service", and laughed like two schoolgirls.

She looked gorgeous. It was amazing what new clothes could do for a woman. "I am going by the BUZZCUTTER and get my hair cut and styled. You want to come?"

"No I have to go do mundane things like cook and clean," Cassie made grotesque faces. "I'm not a lady of leisure like you," and they both laughed.

"Honey you enjoy. You have worn the same dresses for six years. Enjoy!" and she left and Eunice was headed for the beauty salon.

Madeline had taken herself to the salon about the same time. Her reason was to see Jackie and obtain some information that she had.

"Now Jackie, dang it! I've forgotten my newspaper again," Madeline frowned.

"Don't you frown like that your face could get stuck and scare all my customers away!" She giggled and winked at her favorite customer.

"Sign that paper for your coloring and I'll be right back," and she swayed and dipped to the back room to mix the formula while she grabbed her paper from her purse.

"Here honey! Work your crossword puzzle while I do this dye job on you that will make your husband drool ... He is such a TALL fellow..." she winked. "And handsome... yum yum!" Madeline saw the note and a list of names, folded inside the newspaper as usual Jackie had come through.

Jackie continued her banter which distracted the other clients from knowing what was really going on.

"Honey at your wedding I said to myself," she leaned back and said with a wink, cause she knew it was going to put a buzz in this crowd.

"No offense Ms Madeline ... but if he wasn't taken I would have climbed that mountain! What is he ... over six feet tall?"

Madeline was working her puzzle and nodded.

"I would have climbed that ladder to the stars, but I knew he was yours," she was snipping the dead ends from her hair.

"NO NO This old girl don't mess with no other woman's man … when she wears those pointed toe cowboy boots! NO NO…" she was blowing Madeline's hair out by now.

"NO NO NO I ain't fixing to get my pretty little aspirin tablet," she patted her butt. "Kicked by no cowboy boot!" The entire salon was roaring with laughter.

"Now Ms Madeline don't you ever take those cowboy boots off . Do I'll give you a run for the honey!" Jackie scooted behind the counter and grinned.

"Sounds like I better keep my boots on at all times. Don't forget to take your TIP out. Thank you so much for the warning. Trevor may have a problem with me sleeping with my BOOTS on!" and out the door she went to the tune of a buzzing crowd.

That fifty dollar tip had through the years put food on her table. This time she was really worried about her favorite client. This was serious and dangerous. She shivered to think what might happen.

Madeline went by the office where Guy was, "Did you take Kyleigh and Madison by the house?"

"Yes GM," she swatted him with a kiss on his nape.

"I went by and got my hair fixed and you didn't even notice. GS my favorite hair stylist was working," she said.

His feet came off the desk and he was all ears, "What did you learn from her?" he asked.

"I've not opened the information. Didn't want to lose any- thing in the salon or be seen snooping threw it in the parking lot," she frowned. Last thing she needed was to get Jackie hurt.

"Let's see what you got," and he was looking over her shoulder as she unfolded the paper.

He is here. Hal's shop clerk let it slip. My friend says Market street and Howard is a good place to look and the bus station West Main has a man by the name of Claude that is looking for a few bucks to spill his guts.

Take Care!

CHAPTER FOUR

"She is a jewel! Now we can swing by Sophie's. You ready for lunch? And keep those eyes in your head this time," she chastised him. "Last time your eyes were fixed on Sophie's huge breasts and embarrassed me."

"No problem GM. Have you seen my wife's breasts lately, they are enormous," and she swatted him with a magazine.

"Stop that and get in the Mini Cooper before I turn you across my knee," she said.

"Why don't you want me to ride my bike?" he asked.

"Because I can't ride my trike and I am jealous. Trevor said he has to ride with me a couple of times to see how I handle it before I can take it out alone," she showed teeth instead of a smile.

"He is so possessive, you'd think you two were married!" and Guy laughed.

They pulled into the diner and Sophie came to wait on them. She was popping that gum like it was the last piece on earth.

"What'll you folks have?" she was really nervous and it wasn't like Sophie. "Coffee as usual and you, sonny?" She looked around the room smiling while Guy was fixated on her bosom that was falling out of her waitress uniform. "Water."

Guy hadn't a clue that something was not right! Madeline wrote on her napkin, "Keep your gun handy!" and she slid hers out of her handbag into her coat pocket. The cell phone was ringing and she answered.

Then she began giggling hysterically, "Yes dear. Why yes! We are having lunch at the diner. You can come join us, if you'd like!" and she hung up.

Trevor was out the door and three officers with him.

Madeline was in trouble because she never let him say a word.

"Boys my wife is a good PI, but sometimes she oversteps her boundaries. She's in trouble and they may need our help, so you guys follow me and the rest stay here with the women and children."

Sophie brought the coffee and laid extra napkins down.

"Two scrambled eggs and bacon," she looked at what Sophie wrote, He's in the back!

"And you sonny?" Sophie asked winking.

"Three pancakes and bacon," Sophie was popping that gum and placed the order as usual.

Madeline said, "Here you are always spilling stuff on your shirt!" She handed him half the napkins and he read it and looked at the table. He would go to the restroom and investigate.

"Going to wash my hands," he said.

"Sit down silly ... I have my hand sanitizer in my purse!" she reached in and handed it to him, and stared at him and not with her usual sweet smile and then said, "STAY PUT!"

"Thanks!" she kept chitchatting until Trevor came through the door.

"Hi Honey over here!" He kissed her ponytail and sat beside her.

"Sophie can you put those orders in a To Go bag, my big hunk of a man wants to eat at home," she smiled at him.

"How's it going son?" Trevor asked.

"Sure honey I'll be right back," The next napkin said, He left out the backdoor

The coast is clear!

Trevor was going after him but Madeline said, "Don't you dare … take my food. Order your own!"

"OK dear. Get that waitress over here," he ordered and she brought the take-outs and he handed her a fifty extra.

She almost fainted, "You people must come here more often. Enjoy!"

When Madeline got in the Mini, Trevor said, "Get out! Leave it! Get in the station wagon!" They all fit in and were pulling out of the parking lot when her car EXPLODED.

Guy looked at Trevor and they both looked at Madeline.

"See that is why you need to listen to your husband," Trevor called the fire dept. and the police dept.

They were on a mission to get to the office and get that note that was on her desk and go straight home. The men in the car were texting and on cell phones to several agencies to coordinate a capture.

That car was her baby. She loved that Mini, but she was grateful it was a car, and not her grandson. Thank God her grandson was safe. He was going to drive it home and Trevor bless him said, "NO! Son you are coming with us!"

"Must have been a pipe bomb in the tailpipe of the car, it was the only way. This means every car the family gets into can have the same device placed quickly in any parking lot." Guy was on a roll. Hindsight is a teacher!

"Trevor they all need to know now... Crap! We all need to stay with the Feds!"

The men in the car were calling in a few snipers and the A-team and their fortress would be secure.

"We are going on to check out these streets, the woman gave to Mrs. Madeline and we will get him. Till then stay put." The agent had said, "Lonestar's on his way" and Trevor relaxed.

Bruce called Unitus and told him about the car. "Your van needs to come down off the mountain while this is going on. That van is too big and a clear target for a nutcase, if you go into town. So don't think just grab the baby and wife and stay with us!"

"We are on our way," he hung up and looked at Adriana. "We got to stay at Trevor's with the Feds. Can't stay here. The monster blew up Madeline's car … if she had been in it, she would be dead. That's how serious this is. The baby will have many people to hold her and she'll be happy. We have enough diapers for a month."

"I will go on one condition," she stared at him.

"What?" he frowned.

"That you stay put, too …You and Bruce stay out of it! And I mean it … The first time you leave that house, I will walk my baby to the top of this mountain!" she declared.

"Yes dear!" he said anything to get her situated safely. He kissed both of them and they got in the van with that precious dog. He sniffed the van before they got in.

The dog was trained to detect bombs and drugs. What a treasure Unitus thought.

Madeline was trembling when she got home. It really had not set in that she was almost killed, until she saw all her family together. She went to her bedroom and cried. She did not want the rest of the family to see her cry.

Debbie came into her room and hugged her. "It's going to be alright." That is what Madeline had said to her the day she had come to their house seeking safety from the football team.

This was a special moment for both of them and they cried together.

Trevor was in the den and all systems were displaying information and the tracking devices were mind boggling. The A-team had arrived and was assessing the location of the operatives at the addresses. The addresses that Madeline had been given. The info that they got was of great value. Chris's fingerprints were everywhere and being logged for evidence.

Hal's garage was being searched thoroughly for evidence. They had obtained search warrants and the judge gave them carte blanche for anything they needed. The A-Team was going to scour the areas around Chris Shackleford's property. This was not going to be an easy task. They had the bomb squad from Charlotte to bring the tanks that were reinforced to withstand about any kind of explosion.

They were not going to leave his house standing. They would pick it apart. If he was there, they would find him.

He and his accomplices were in the woods watching the Feds rip his place apart and he launched a rocket to strike the house. "Be damn if they will go through my things!"

He had Jung's goons with him and they sped away and then slowed on the highway. They looked like the average Chinese couple out on the freeway for a Sunday afternoon spin. They were on their way to New York to regroup and better plan how to take the Smiths out.

"We underestimated the hicks and you ... Chris Shackleford ain't worth a dime. Jung will know it before the day is done."

"Mess with me and I'll blow this car up. He opened his shirt and he was wired with a bomb. I will get the job done, if it kills me. I always have and always will. So turn this car around you fools." That's what they did.

Eunice had returned to find Jennifer, her daughter and her friend in the driveway. She ran around the car and hugged her mother and introduced her friend as Queen La Feather. She was an Afro-American and had the most sophisticated air about her. She spoke perfect English and Eunice was enthralled at what Jennifer was up to. Something just didn't feel right!

"Yes, we are lesbians and I hate I have to tell you like this and upset you before Corey's graduation. You needed to know! Jason and Corey will NOT know unless you tell them MOM. Mom are you okay?"

Eunice was in shock, but answered. "Get the stuff out of the car, Jennifer." It maybe just a phase that she is going through. So Eunice don't get upset, she told herself. You have Corey and Jason to think of and murder was not on Corey's graduation gift list. She smiled at the girls who were just talking up a storm.

"Mom I love your new clothes. Have you lost weight? What's up?" Jennifer was prying.

"I just got a few things that I have been needing and some-thing special for Corey's graduation. I am so glad to meet you Queen and make yourself at home. Jennifer unpack your suitcase and wash things, if you need to." She went into her bedroom and started hanging up her clothes when she heard Jason and Corey coming in the backdoor.

She waited until she heard them introducing themselves.

Corey picked up on the situation, but little brother was clueless.

Corey asked, "What did mom say?"

"Nothing yet! We are of age, so shut your face!" Jennifer was showing off. "How'd you do at school this year? Any chance you're going to summer school?"

"Not with a 4.0 Yes ... I applied myself this year. So feel free to pat me on the back!" Jennifer hugged him and Queen shook his hand real hard.

Eunice said that was a good thing, all were getting along.

She would look at it as if she was adopting another child.

The graduation was nice and Corey looked so handsome, more like his father everyday.

Eunice almost cried and Jason said, "Why are you sad mama? You said this was a happy day!" and she told him, "I am very happy ... but sometimes people cry happy tears!"

"Okay as long as you are happy you can kiss me. None of my friends are here, so it's okay!" He knew if she got a kiss, she'd stop that crying.

She kissed him and said, "Now you got to work hard so you can get one of those hats."

"They're no good, I don't want one. Did you see them all throw them away and let them fall on the ground," Jason said.

Eunice looked so nice that three service men had spoke to her. She could not remember when a man had spoke unless his wife spoke first. Probably being polite, but it felt good.

Corey and Ellen were kissing for all to see. They both had their graduation robes on, his hands were out of sight in hers.

"We can get jobs and get married anytime you say Ellen," Corey told her.

"We will have plenty time now that we have graduated. We can take it slow and do it right!" Ellen was going to have to think for the both of them because Corey had one thing on his mind.

"Your mom is coming our way," Ellen said.

"I got this big robe on, don't worry," Corey was really not hiding a thing from his Mom.

She was going to have to have the father-son talk with him. She looked at the sky and said, "You should be here for this one."

The crowd was taking pictures so she asked Jennifer if she would get some with her camera.

She did and they all posed and it was a good day for the sun was shining on the football field.

Eunice had not been on this field since her daughter Coraine had died at the hands of the FOOTBALL TEAM. She hated the sight of it until today. For Corey she came … to salute his day!

No one had thought of her poor Coraine. She knew Debbie and Tate would, but they could not be here. She loved those two kids, also. She must give them a call and send them a picture … like they had asked of her.

CHAPTER FIVE

Cassie saw Eunice and she waved her over. "I have set you up for this week-end with Cpl. Roger Mc Mahon. His wife died three years ago. He is hilarious. A laugh a minute, if you don't hit it off, the girls and I will go scouting for another. Don't sweat it just have fun! He will pick you up at six PM on Saturday. Call me afterward."

"I can't believe you did this while Jennifer is home, but okay. Thanks! I'll call you!"

"Don't worry Mom! Queen and I are out of here tomorrow. It is time you dated. You have my blessing and write me anytime with the details." Jennifer hugged her mom.

Eunice checked with Corey, "What are you doing Saturday night?"

"Going out with Ellen as usual. Why?" Corey asked.

"I have a date," she said nervously.

"You have a what?" Corey stood in front of the sink with his mouth wide open.

"Shut your mouth before a fly goes in there. I know Cassie has set me up and I said okay. I maybe back within an hour. If longer I will call," she said biting the inside of her lip.

"I'll call Ellen, of course we will Mom," Corey had not seen her go out of this house in six years at night with anyone. It was about time. Soon he hoped, he and Ellen would be get-ting married and he had not talked to his mom about that yet.

Kyleigh and Beatrice agreed it was nice to be able to talk and the kiddos could play together. The nanny and house-keeper were taking a week's vacation. They did not want them in the middle of this chaos.

Everyone was helping everyone.

Adriana and Unitus were learning all sorts of useful stuff. Techniques and shortcuts to help them with little Angel. Bruce and Jana were observant so they could help any of the new mothers and fathers.

Bruce had given his loyal ninjas time off, also. The Feds were informed how valuable these two men had been in their masks. They had taken the masks off, and their true identity revealed. Per protocol, they still had to be cleared. They were and Bruce assured them that they would remain on the payroll.

While the family stayed in one place, the Feds were in and out. Trevor was with them most of the time at the command center.

Still no word on the whereabouts of Chris.

The news team was getting involved as word came that Marcus Buchanan, the billionaire had arrived at the Charlotte Airport and his entourage consist of ten body guards. They had his limo waiting and all black SUV s. They went directly to Trevor's and were filled in on the status of the situation.

Adriana hugged her daddy and Unitus shook his hand and the baby was sleeping. They sat and talked. One of the

Feds took the men over to Madeline's old house and they settled in to their lodging. These men were not only body guards, but experts in defusing explosives. They could use their undercover skills to penetrate any operation around the world and would flush out the enemy and take them out. Their goal as well as the FBI and CIA was to take the organization out that hired this Chris Shackleford.

The problem with a small town was where everyone knew everybody and any new face stuck out like a sore thumb. This could take time for them to establish themselves in the community. They had researched on the plane what the locals culture was and who were the leaders in the community.

Roscoe introduced them to the local police department and his security staff. They went over to the FOREMOST CONSTRUCTION COMPANY and introduced him to Frankie and Lefty. Lefty was anxious to help give them the lowdown on Chris. Also he gave them names of people that also could brief them on everything about Chris and his habits.

Marcus had gone with them there to this company to set up the construction of his new home and he had gone by city hall. The development proposal for the highrise hotel and casino had been approved.

Yes, it was met with much excitement and an emergency Board Meeting was held within the hour. All clearance to go forward was in writing with the lawyers Royster Martin & Royster were present to oversee the contracts and make sure they were legally binding. Permits were already applied for.

He had purchased the land on his last visit. It was just a matter of Marcus writing the check for the construction to begin. He would go this afternoon to the law offices and finalize the morning's arrangements and set them into motion.

Eunice had not liked her date on Saturday with the corporal. He was obnoxious and his hands were everywhere. It was clear to her that he thought because she had been alone for six years that she would be starved for sex. She put him in his place by slapping him in public and made her escape via taxi to her home. Immediately she called Cassie and gave her a piece of her mind.

Corey had to cover Jason's ears and Ellen distracted him by giving him a listen on her Bose headphones of today's music which he was into the pop music.

Eunice went straight to her room and stayed there. She was so humiliated. She hung her beautiful dress up and went to bed without saying goodnight to anyone.

Corey and Ellen played Monopoly with Jason until he yawned and fell asleep on the couch.

Monday Eunice decided to wear one of her new dresses and she applied her makeup as the woman in the hair salon had suggested for the sleek "office" look. Her hair had held the style all weekend which she was grateful.

When she walked in the law office, the staff came rushing and asked, "May I help you, ma'am?"

She turned around and her boss nearly fainted, "Eunice you look wonderful! This is the way a receptionist should look especially today."What's so special about today?" she was putting her personal items into her desk drawer.

"I guess you haven't heard," Theresa said. "That billionaire whose daughter is the District Attorney is here. His name is Marcus Buchanan. He is coming in this afternoon to sign some papers. Now you put that pretty lipstick on before he comes in. You look fabulous."

"Theresa for once could you say something nice about my work," never had Eunice talked back to her that way. She was just tired of people running all over her.

Theresa walked away with a smirk on her face.

Eunice knew she would pay for that comment, but it made her feel good so she smiled all morning and worked through lunch and caught up. No one would have anything negative to say to her. She put on the dang lipstick as her boss requested and she was smiling when Marcus came through the door.

"This is what I like a beautiful woman waiting to greet me," and he gave her a wink.

She frowned and asked, "May I help you Mr .... ?"

"Buchanan, my dear," he was still standing.

"And whom would you like to see?" she asked and he looked puzzled.

He was so use to people falling at his feet and now this gorgeous lady was not.

"Royster Martin & Royster ma'am," he was intrigued.

"Which one of the three, do you want to see?" and she gave him a great big smile.

He turned his head to the side, "You really have no idea who I am do you? I would like to see the entire firm ..." and then he smiled.

"Mr Buchanan ... if you will please have a seat, I will let them know you are here," she pressed the intercom and told them. Marcus had sat down staring at her.

She had started typing as if he was not even in the room, and the lawyers came barreling through the door. All three trying to get through the door at the same time, "Marcus we are so sorry!" Turning to Eunice, "You should have shown Mr. Buchanan in ... as soon as he got here!"

She stood all five foot two of her in a navy dress and red heels with red lipstick to match, and leaned on her desk.

"These gentlemen failed to tell me you were special, Mr. Buchanan. I do apologize. It won't happen again."

She got her purse out of the drawer and added, "I am going on my lunch break. I will be gone for one hour. Please have Theresa to see to all of Mr. Buchanan's needs. She smiled sweetly at him and went through the door with the phone ringing off the hook. That should fix Miss Theresa's goose. She may not have a job when she got back, but she sure did feel damn good. She walked around for an hour refusing to go back one minute earlier.

"Do come into my office Marcus. I will deal with my receptionist when she returns. Theresa answer that phone!"

"She did nothing to apologize for. You can't expect your employee as you put it ... to read your mind. So when I come again. SHE will know who I am, and she HAD BETTER be sitting behind that desk."

Marcus walked into the private office with Royster Martin & Royster hovering behind him.

"She will, sir. She will," Royster was groveling at his feet.

He was gone when she got back and true to form Theresa was furious. She just went about typing and answering the phone like no one was going to unnerve her today.

Marcus had had the chauffeur to wait by the corner, so he could watch this receptionist swing her pocketbook and bounce down the sidewalk. It looked like she was humming something. She was ordinary but interesting, I bet she is dynamite in bed and she is my size.

He grinned, "Have them send that receptionist a dozen red roses from me and I will personally sign the card. Get her name."

I want her to truly remember me. I can see her smiling while she is smelling the fragrance of the roses. Dang this is the first time I have felt this alive in years. I got to focus on my grand baby, now get it together Marcus, he told himself.

CHAPTER SIX

This little town was buzzing because the news people had invaded. They were broadcasting Chris Shackleford's picture every hour with the caption:

THIS MAN IS ARMED AND DANGEROUS
If you see him call 1-800-404-1111 or
go to your local police station.
All tips will remain anonymous!
THERE IS A REWARD for information leading
to his capture $10,000.00

Roscoe and Guy wanted to help as did Bruce and Unitus, but that was not going to happen. The wives had them within eye view at all times.

"What you say we play a little poker?" and he said very low "and pretend we are betting big bucks. Just to see how long it takes for them to peck, peck, peck their way into our game."

Tate came in and joined, "This is our secret," and they told him to bet big and see if his new bride would respond

like the rest and peck, peck, peck. "Then you will know …
you are truly one of us, Tate," Roscoe said.

Without being able to go to the grocery store themselves,
they had groceries delivered by a reliable source and the Feds
checked the vehicles at the checkpoint and the dogs sniffed
the bottom of all the grocery bags. Everything was good.

Trevor said, "Anyone seen Lonestar yet? He is one
tracking man. You know he and I served together. I've
always trusted him with my life so now he will be amazed,
at how many lives he can save. He does love a challenge."
Into the com-mand center which was Trevor's office, walked
Lonestar.

"You are really singing my praises and I appreciate
it …but I do this out of love. No recognition is needed. The
quieter about me, the better I like it."

Trevor hugged him and locked hands with a firm shake.

"Here's what I know...The Japanese kingpin JUNG has
had a grudge against Bruce for breaking up his lucrative
smuggling business. Jared Banks was his main man in
Dallas. Word is in Chinatown that he hired Shackleford
and has put a lot into the breaking him out of prison," he
was walking around the room.

"Chris I am told is wearing a bomb on his person, and
is willing to die, if he cannot complete his mission. So if he
is seen, we can take him out with one shot … but the blast
may injury many. He may decide to cling to people or jump
into a crowd. He is a lunatic that likes to kill as many people
as he can at one time." Trevor was continuing to walk and
observe people.

"If you can flush him out into an open area. I got him,"
Lonestar never said what he did not mean. Then he was gone.

"He is going to mingle with the people. He'll be back."

The women did disrupt the poker game, and all they had to say was "let's eat!" They ate at the long dining room table and Trevor's specialty is grace, "Thankful that my family is safe!"

Eunice went in to work Tuesday morning and there were roses on her desk. She smelled of them. They must be for someone in the back. I'd better read the card and take them to whomever.

Her eyes were getting bigger and bigger as she read the card, "Just wanted you to remember my name, Marcus Buchanan." She looked around as if this man was going to pop out from the wall.

She sat and looked around to see if anyone else saw them and they were standing peeping around the corner, all scared to see what kind of mood she would be in, and to see what outfit she was wearing. Theresa was quite nice to her today!

Royster must have told her to shut her trap and she was answering the phone smiling. "Royster Martin & Royster, How may I help you? This is Eunice speaking."

"Did you get my flowers, my dear?" Marcus inquired.

"If this is Mr Buchanan I certainly did, and they are just beautiful. Thank you, that was very kind!"

"Marcus, please. Call me Marcus. I noticed you didn't have a wedding band on," he stated.

"No, I am a widow," Eunice said lowly.

"Would you like to have dinner with me at THE INN tonight?" Marcus asked.

"I'm sorry I can't! It is a school night and my twelve year old cannot be left alone. Perhaps another time," she had refused.

"Why don't I pick you both up around seven?" he stated.

"I am sorry, but I can't," she was adamant.

"Or just don't want to spend time with me?" he questioned.

"No No, that is not it at all. The other reason is it's against company policy to date clients. I will just be truthful with you. Don't want you to think I don't want to because I do," Eunice was blushing everyone was crowding around.

"I will have a talk with your boss now put him on the line," Marcus had NEVER been turned down for a dinner date.

"Royster … I have ask your receptionist out for dinner. She says it is against company policy. Could there be an exception made on my behalf," Buchanan was going to get his way about everything.

"Of course! Yes, of course I will talk with her, now," Royster hung up.

Eunice was typing away when Royster came out of his office frowning, "Ahem … Eunice may I talk to you?"

"But of course, what about?" she was going to play dumb.

"He says company policy forbids dating clients and this is true, but Mr Buchanan can mean millions to this law firm. So you have my permission to dine with him. In fact, please dine with him. If you need a new outfit put it one on my account! OK?"

"OK. How much can I spend, sir?" she giggled.

"Whatever you need, get it and go home for the rest of the day. He will meet you at the restaurant at 7:00pm. Now go!"

She took her roses and ran out the door.

She bought her the most expensive dress and pair of heels in the department store and a sexy lingerie set.

She had to call Cassie. "I can't believe what has happened. I just bought a $600 dress and undies and $300 on shoes."

Cassie said, "You have loss your mind! You got to return it!

You have gone shopping CRAZY!"

"I can't my boss insisted," Eunice was playing with her.

"So you are having an affair with one of those lawyers. Which one? Oh let me guess," Cassie was saying, "eenie, meanie, mi....."

"Stop! I would never have an affair with a married man," Eunice said. "Tsk tsk on you, Cassie!"

"OK tell all," Cassie was eager to hear. "This better be good!"

"I got a dozen red roses today," Eunice was going to make her pop her cork.

"From whom? Tell me! Tell me!" Cassie was salivating.

"From the same guy I am going out with tonight that my boss bought the dress for me to wear, that is!...... If you will watch Jason for me?'

"Who and yes I will?" Cassie knew it wasn't the Cpl.

"Marcus Buchanan!" Eunice said softly.

"The billionaire?" Cassie SCREAMED.

"Yes...." she said and heard a thud.

"Cassie did you hurt yourself?" Eunice knew she stumbled.

"Not much and to think, I got you all dolled up and this is what happens!" \She screamed, "I am so happy for you!"

"It is just a dinner, nothing more. Nothing less. I admit I am excited. I just hope I don't slap him, too!" she laughed.

"Roscoe, honey we have to go to the house and get a few things for the girls. The boys are fine. We can take

Dynamite and a few men, and I can wash some clothes. Since we don't have a housekeeper or a nanny," she gave him those sad puppy dog eyes.

He agreed and Trevor said, "I wish you wouldn't, let Lonestar get back before you make any moves!"

Roscoe told Beatrice, "It's not safe yet! Maybe in about a week. Trevor wants us here. I told him we are here for the duration."

"The housekeeper and nanny can come here during the day. GM says the laundry room is huge and you are welcome to use anything as we would, if they were staying with us honey," Roscoe reassured her.

"Okay I'll call Mrs B, but we have to get another nanny. Yes dear! She quit, that week off must have been the deciding factor. I'll let Kyleigh pick you another one," she grinned.

Roscoe knew what that meant, no young chickadees in his house and he grinned back, "Sounds good, dear!"

The women were enjoying having someone to do the chores with and play with all the babies. Most of all Madeline was delighted to have a house full. "This house has been quiet for too long. It was just what I needed."

One of the Feds went to each house Roscoe's, Guy's, and Unitus's every day taking one of the bomb sniffing dogs.

Today the dog pushed a button at Roscoe's. THAT meant with all the security, a weasel had planted a bomb. Trevor looked at Roscoe, "See why I didn't want you going?" and he said, "We will see who's fingerprints are there."

The bomb squad had dismantled the bomb that was under the house near the bedroom where Roscoe slept. He could not tell Beatrice. Trevor said that was a good idea.

The prints were Chris's, and Lonestar was back to say he had located him, but "he was too close to people." He dropped a chip in his pocket. Lonestar was a good picket-pocket, and also could plant things without a person knowing it. "We will be able to pinpoint where he is … if he has that coat on."

Trevor said, "You were too close my friend. He could have pulled the cord on his bomb vest and killed my best friend. Get him, but don't get hurt. Good friends are HARD to find!"

"I will track him and get him. You people stay put," Lonestar motioned for three of the agents to go with him.

Now there were four men assigned to each house to have all directions monitored at all times. They had video cams, but Chris had been doing this kind of meanness for many years. It wasn't a system that he didn't know how to cut the right wire to disable it. Sometimes humans can outdo a machine, and this was one example.

PART THIRTEEN

CHAPTER ONE

Marcus had invited Madeline and Trevor to dine with him and a lady friend at THE INN. It was clearly going to make Trevor tense. Since Marcus had brought a small army to help and he was staying with them, they felt obligated to go. The limo had two guards and there was a car in front and a car in back. Each having a dog inside, to check cars and people.

They were escorted inside and taken to the private dining room in the back. Marcus told the hostess to please bring the female that was joining them in here.

After ten minutes and drinks were brought to the table, he told the waiter they would wait. He did not like to be kept waiting. So they engaged in small talk. Eunice was escorted to their table and she looked ravishing.

She was wearing a stunning pale pink creation by Vera Wang and matching shoes with a white shawl. Marcus took her hand and kissed it and helped her be seated.

He was about to introduce her and Madeline said, "You look gorgeous, Eunice. I love that dress," and they started talking. Completely ignoring the men. Trevor looked at the ceiling. "You want to go to the bar for a moment or two?

They have a lot to catch up on," and they excused themselves. They asked the ladies to order their meal for them.

"Where did you meet Eunice, Marcus?" Trevor was dying to know because they made a cute couple both being short.

"She was at the law office and we started talking. She challenges me and that hasn't happened in a long while."

"Yeah, Madeline challenges me and that is hard to find. I notice you and she are also about eye to eye like me and Madeline. That is hard to find, too."

"She says she is a widow. Did you know her husband?" Marcus was trying to get information that would help him talk to her sensitive side.

"No I never met him. He was a military man and died on a mission six years ago … leaving her with four children to raise and she has done a good job."

"Four?" Marcus took a chug of bourbon, instead of a sip.

"Marcus relax! They have all graduated, but one. I think he is thirteen. I talk too much!" then he took a chug of brandy.

"We better get back before they start gnawing the table legs," Marcus said walking fast to keep up with Trevor.

Trevor said softly, "Or we might get drunk! I haven't eaten since breakfast."

"Sorry … we had a lot to catch up on!" said Marcus and that made Eunice smile.

"We did also. We ordered Trevor's favorite. I had no idea what you would like. Tell me what you like," Eunice was gazing into Marcus's eyes and he was lost for a minute.

"Anything you like … I like," Marcus could not believe he said that, it must be the bourbon.

Trevor whispered to Madeline, "Marcus has met his match, mark my word," and winked.

"I think you are right," Madeline said to Trevor looking into his eyes. "So glad I have my soul-mate!" he kissed her hand.

"What did you girls order us? I am curious to find out what whet your appetite Eunice?" Marcus patted her hand and she put it in her lap.

"My napkin was falling. I like roast beef and mash potatoes and string beans with cornbread. It's a simple meal. I like things simple. Is that okay with you?"

He grinned, "Perfect. A southern belle who likes southern cooking. That's a perfect combination! I fell in love .... last visit with the southern food here at this restaurant." He said, "I hope the food comes soon before I make a fool of myself." He was stroking her hand.

"Me, too! So I don't have to slap you!" she laughed.

His mouth fell open and he said, "Why would you want to do a thing like that?" staring into her eyes. Trying to focus on her mouth not her cleavage, but the boobs won.

She said, "Well when I have had too much to drink my girlfriend will give me a slap and it brings me right around!"

The waiter was serving their meal by then.

"Have no fear! Eunice I will take a swat at him, if he gets out of hand." Trevor said.

"They are okay Eunice. I will slug them both," Madeline said and they all burst out laughing.

"I love this town. I love these people. That's why I am moving here, Honey!" looking at Eunice.

Eunice was eating her beef and commenting on it. "Just needs a touch of salt, don't you agreed, dear?" talking to Madeline.

231

But Marcus looked at Eunice as if he could eat her alive, "I like the sound of that. Trevor help me pick her out a ring tomorrow. I don't have my phone with me to make a note. It is always going off when I am eating. Tonight my dear, you have my full attention!"

"That's it, Marcus! The only way to dine is enjoy your food and enjoy the company you are with. Why? Because it is like you are eating alone, otherwise. Don't call. Don't ask. I want 100 % attention when I eat out. How about you Madeline?"

"Well said Sister!" and she looked from Trevor to Marcus.

"Is that clear, gentlemen? The women have spoken and it shall be done!"

They raised their glasses and Marcus did not know what they were doing, but he joined in. "Here! Here!"

Eunice leaned over to whisper to Marcus, and he was scooting his chair nearer to hear, "That's their family's special cheer. They adopted my nephew, and he told me before the Christmas dinner that they would be doing it, and for me to join in."

"Thank you my lovely, for sharing that. So Tate is your nephew, he is a fine young man. I am staying there and now I can break it to him ... that we are dating or do you prefer to tell him?" Marcus was swooning over her.

Madeline said, "She is going to smack him, Trevor."

"Marcus this is a dinner that I have truly enjoyed, but nothing more. I must be going. I did not check the time. I have to be going, Goodnight all!" She was out the door.

Madeline spoke to the guard, "Get the dog and check her car" she told him. Eunice waved to Madeline, and got in the car and a arm came around her neck................

"Hi sis! Long time no see!" She screamed and the dog was through the window and the guard grabbed Eunice. Then Lonestar was on the roof, and he shot CHRIS IN THE TEMPLE and he didn't have time to pull the cord to detonate the vest. The vest had to be removed by the bomb squad, so the entire restaurant had to be evacuated.

Trevor was shaking Lonestar's hand and Marcus had his arms around Eunice holding her. Held her without talking.

Madeline was on the phone with Roscoe, and he would tell the others.

"Marcus can you take me home before the news people get here................... I can't drive right now," she was trembling uncontrollably. He walked her to the white limo and con-tinued to hold her.

"I have to call Cassie before she or my sons hears it on the news." Madeline was with them and she called Cassie.

"Cassie can you pack a few things for Eunice and Jason and we will be by in a few. She doesn't need to be there. The news people will be there wanting to interview her, and I can't let it happen. She is in no condition to talk about it. She will be at our house. If Corey wants to come tell him to hurry and he can ride with Jason."

Trevor shook his head, "That's a good idea! I have to stay here to help Lonestar and the agents wrap this up and then I'll be home."

The limo sped away to Eunice's address. Corey and Jason got in with the large suitcase. They were looking at this strange man with his arms around their mother.

No one said anything until they got to Southfork and everyone was piling out down the staircase. Corey and Jason had been there for Christmas, so pretty much knew where everything was.

Madeline said, "Finally it is over and we can all get back to normal … whatever that is."

Adriana was looking at her father holding Eunice, and she smiled at Unitus who was rocking the baby in his arms.

"Honey you ready to climb this mountain?" Unitus asked.

"Let Trevor get back, and then I would love to climb your mountain?" He almost dropped the baby.

"Let me hold her. You get so excited at the least little thing!" and she grinned.

Roscoe and Beatrice had started to pack their stuff and Beatrice was calling Mrs. B to come to their house tomorrow morning.

Kyleigh and Madison were playing with the babies while Guy packed the few things that they had brought. They still had clothes here from Dallas. The things that Kyleigh had BAD memories wearing. She had no bad memories here and had been wearing everything, and she smiled at Guy.

Tate was holding Debbie. She could now relax. His father was dead. Thank God … he was dead and would never hurt Adam or himself ever again. Aunt Eunice was almost killed.

He would hug her when that man let her go.

Tate asked Corey, "Who is that man hugging Aunt Eunice?"

"He's the billionaire Marcus Buchanan. He's Adriana's dad."

"Oh … I was wondering why no one was breaking them up especially you and Jason." "Nah, she told us they were going out to eat, but I never thought their first date would end like this."

Jason was playing the Nintendo game and suddenly started pulling on Corey's arm.

"I don't have to go to school tomorrow, do I?" Jason was almost turning cartwheels in the game room. "Yes" pulling his fist out of the air and to his body, as if he was doing a karate move.

"Where are we sleeping? In here would be fine," Jason wanted to play games all night.

"We'll see what mom says, if that man ever takes his hands off her. They're stuck like glue." Jason said.

"He is comforting her because she was almost killed tonight. You are old enough to know the truth. You'll be fourteen in a few months." Corey saw his little brother start crying, he had no idea what his mother had been through. Cassie didn't tell him. Corey hugged him, "she's fine. She's fine."

Jason went and hugged his mother as did Corey.

"Thank you Mr Buchanan for taking care of our mother," Corey said.

Jason said, "Thanks!"

Marcus patted both the boys on the back and gave them a big hug.

Eunice was smiling. Seeing her boys bond with Marcus was a happy moment.

She had to talk to Madeline, something just hit her.

"I am going crazy... because Chris was my brother, they wouldn't put my name in the paper. His military service will bury him. Right?" she was frantic and pale.

Madeline was not sure, but she was afraid the reporter had already got that information. "Trevor can answer that question when he gets home or tomorrow we can ask him. But Tate's will definitely be in there unless a miracle happens.

She went to her room and closed the door and called Trevor.

"Honey I need a favor. Please sit down," she said.

"Tell me they won't put Tate's name in the newspaper. Tell me they won't put Eunice's name in the paper. Will they send him back to the prison that he broke out of for them to bury him?" Then she took a deep breath and sighed.

"I'll see what I can do, calm down and keep everyone calm."

Bruce was talking to Unitus, "Everyone is forgetting that the KINGPIN can hire someone else, and you and I know it."

CHAPTER TWO

Trevor called his cousin to have Chris Shackleford the escapee brought back to his PRISON and buried.

"You owe me Warden Porter. You and your talk of how secure your prison was and then this. What you have put my family through. You come get him … today!"

Bruce had gone with Unitus to find Trevor. The Feds were still there and Trevor was talking to Lonestar.

"Can we all go to Madeline's old house? Or to GM & GS Private Investigation Service office? We will still need all of you guys."

"Taking out Chris is good … but Jung will hire someone else. He wants me bad, and now he wants my family. He has lost more and more. The money he spent on Chris will be eating a hole in his soul about now."

"Unitus and I have fought this man for years. Unitus has a new baby and I cannot definitely put myself out there. As much as he wants to, and I am standing trial. If I fart wrong, they will have me put back for JUNG to get me in prison."

"I am begging for my family. This monster is Chris's equal in every way. He has no regard for human life. There it is in a nut shell. I have two ninjas with me that maybe able to shed more light. They can infiltrate back into Jung's environment where we cannot. We would stick out like a sore thumb."

"If there are any Japenese within either agency, they would also be useful. I'm just throwing things out for you 'all to coordinate. I have not talked to Roscoe and Guy, just wanted them to get one good night sleep before I remind them. Thanks for all you have done." Bruce said.

Unitus and Bruce rode back with several of the Feds. Trevor stayed with Lonestar, "Man you have to come home and stay with us."

"You have a house full and I am staying over at the Best Western. I'll wait around till I find out what the plan is," Lonestar crossed his arms.

Trevor said, "Everyone has headed home to their house. No excuse for you to stay in a motel. I see you are determined to stay where it is quiet!" and he laughed.

"Talk tomorrow!" and he caught the last of the men going back to the ranch. The rest was going to Madeline's old house.

Madeline and Debbie were getting Eunice and the boys settled, and she told Eunice not to worry that Trevor was handling what we talked about earlier. She sighed and hugged her.

Marcus was sitting by the fire pit gazing at the stars talking with Tate.

"You have come into the best family on the east coast. Once I get my place built you can come over and play some golf with me. What you studying in college?" Marcus asked.

"Business management and computers ... haven't decided what I will major in. I just am so thankful for Trevor and Ms Madeline!"

Marcus said, "Computers are where the money is ... it is very competitive. The main thing is do what you enjoy doing and you will succeed."

"A very wise man said that Tate," Trevor had finally got home.

"The women and boys have gone to bed. Bruce and Unitus have gone to get their wives settled. I don't expect for them to pop back out," Marcus said.

"What an evening you have had my friend. The first date and the fireworks were bursting in air," Trevor said.

"Well I'll say goodnight and thank you both for saving my aunt," Tate went off to his room and into Debbie's arms.

"That boy has many emotions going on in his head tonight, thank you for keeping him company and I am going to say goodnight, too. I've got a big meeting in the morning. Make yourself at home," Trevor said.

Marcus answered, "Thanks ... it has been unforgettable! We must do it again, have dinner together that is..." and he laughed.

"I'm going to bed soon ... the moon over the mountains is just so magnificent. I've never TAKEN time to see it clearly until tonight! Goodnight."

Jana was not going to let Bruce out of her sight. She had bought a sexy lingerie outfit meant to entice him, and he fell asleep. "Poor baby... trying to play opossum... let me see if ... this will awaken you!" She loved to taste ... immediately he was returning the favor.

Beatrice was so glad to be home in her own bed with all four kids asleep and she began snoring, before Roscoe finished his shower. She was exhausted and he didn't wake her.

Adriana and Unitus were looking at the moon and she was climbing the mountain. The baby was sleeping and the monitor was quiet. "So glad to be home" she whispered.

Tate was not talking and Debbie just laid watching his chest rise and fall. He will when he is ready, she said to herself.

Corey and Jason did talk some about their father and about Mr. Buchanan, but soon they were both asleep. Eunice had just left checking on them, and was returning to her own room, when she saw Marcus coming toward her.

"If you can't sleep, we could talk?" he offered.

"I definitely can't sleep. Every time I have tried … I feel his arm around my throat." Eunice said softly.

"Come let's walk to the glider, out back the view of the moon over the mountains and it reflecting on the lake, is breathtaking."

She agreed. It was beautiful. So they sat and didn't need to talk. He wanted to hold her, but instead just held her hand. He said to himself you have to go slow or she will reject you.

Money doesn't mean a thing to this woman. Peace of mind is what money cannot buy. She said goodnight and thanked him for tonight and she went to her room, and he to his.

Trevor and Madeline were sound asleep now that the house was quiet, and the Feds were still here watching over them.

The morning brought a new hustle and bustle to this house. Trevor had fed the horses and dogs, and went back in to eat the large breakfast Madeline had cooked him. She kissed him before sitting down, "I know you have things to do with your team, but give me a call off and on today! Just to let me know … what's going on that way … I won't pay you a visit."

"I will it is going to be busy. I will say the battle has not been won until ALL are behind bars. I got to go. I'll take the coffee with me and the egg sandwich. Love you!" out the door he went.

She stood at the door and watched him and the others get into the limo with its escorts. Eunice and the boys came around the corner and Eunice smiled. She helped to fix them a nice breakfast, too.

"You boys can go see the horses if you like. The dogs will follow you and keep you safe, but today neither of you can leave here. The news people will be everywhere. Our security men should keep them away from getting down this long road. Go to the game room anytime and the movie room, it's going to be a long day!"

"You are too good to them. They will never want to go home," Jason came and hugged his mom as did Corey.

"You just sit and rest. I'll keep up with Jason," Corey said.

Marcus came around the corner and Eunice poured him some coffee. She was still in her quaint robe.

"Thank you, my dear! Good morning to both of you pretty ladies. Someone has cooked a feast here," eggs, bacon, grits, sliced fruit and three different breads were prepared.

"Help yourself. I confess it was Debbie, she loves to cook and is going to culinary school part-time to be a chef.

Anyways I did fix the coffee," Madeline smiled.

"And it is mighty good," Eunice said and sipped hers.

"Feels weird! Not going to classes, but I know better," Tate said as he came in yawning. Debbie will be out in a minute. Didn't she do a good job?"

Debbie came in dressed in jeans with an apron around her.

"She's the best!" Madeline said. Everyone held up their cups and said, "Here! Here" in unison and Marcus was chuckling and joining in.

"Mighty good girlie! When I get the hotel built, I'm going to need a good chef. So you can keep on practicing on me until then, I'll make a spot for you!" Marcus meant what he said.

She was beaming and kissed Marcus on the cheek and sat beside Tate. Tate said, "You have made Debbie's day. Thank you, sir," then he dug into the scrambled eggs.

"She just made my day, son. Anyone else?" pointing to his cheek for another kiss.

Eunice smiled, but did not move. Madeline blew him an air kiss and he caught it and put it in his pocket, "Can't have Trevor mad at me, so I'll save that one."

"How are you feeling this morning?" Looking at Eunice and smiling.

"I feel humble and very thankful to have such good friends to come to my aid when I really needed them," Eunice said.

Jason came running and said, "Come on you 'all have got to see this on TV," pulling on Eunice to get her to stand.

"Wait Jason. I got it right here," Madeline pushed a button and the chalkboard in the kitchen raised up to reveal a TV in the wall. She turned it on, and the volume up when she found the local station.

It was a mob scene. A real three-ring circus, "We are at the crime site where Chris Shackleford, the school bus bomber had escaped from a Georgia prison where he was serving a life sentence for murder. He was taken down by a government sniper with one shot at the local restaurant THE INN. He was wearing a bomb vest strapped to his chest. He was going to attempt to murder family members of the Smith and Porter families. The patriarch of the family Mr Trevor Porter has agreed to meet with us on behalf of his family. He requests privacy for them after this tragic event." The reporter continued to interview him on camera.

Madeline did not want the kids to witness anything else so she pressed the button and the chalkboard came down.

"Trevor handled it to keep your names out and the prison will bury him. Trevor's cousin the warden agreed to do this. It will just take a couple days to clear this up. I want you all to stay put here. I can't have my house empty all of a sudden. You 'all must keep Trevor and I company."

They were all talking and laughing when HER boys came in to see Trevor. "He's on TV! You two can go and watch TV or you can sit down and eat and wait. Don't go to town!"

Lonestar had met Haruto at the Best Western and they started talking about Bruce and Trevor. "Want to go over to McDonald's and talk or anywhere in private?" Haruto asked.

"Yes, the park is just around the corner. Usually has a bunch of punks and that is why very few people won't go there. I think you and I are capable of teaching them a lesson or two … if we have to," Lonestar said.

"You are right. I have had a few days off and I don't want to get rusty," Haruto grinned which was rare. His wife appeared and he told her in Japanese. "It is business to go back in and that this man Lonestar is Trevor's friend," she bowed and went to her room.

They walked and did little talking and were observing their environment. At the picnic table, they sat on top with their backs touching. So that every aspect of the park was visible to one or the other at all times, while they talked.

"We got Shackleford. I guess you saw it on TV," Lonestar said whittling a twig with his switchblade knife. His eyes were surveying the grounds.

"Yes, I saw. Good shot. There's something on your mind. Spill it," Haruto didn't like to beat around the bush. He too, was scanning the park area.

"Jung hired Shackleford. He has to be angry with the waste of his time and his money by now. Do you know any of his people and do you think they are here?" Lonestar put it out there. Trusting Trevor and Bruce on this one.

"Bruce called me and said you are to be trusted or we would not be sitting here. Jung is a huge kingpin. Just to know of him means your life is in jeopardy. I know his pattern and I will be able to recognize his men when they come. They will not come till this town quietens, and the news media goes away. That is a given. They will sneak in, do their job, and leave. These hicks will not know what hit them … Unless you and I stay and help them," Haruto's expression and voice tone never changed.

"I will stay. Trevor was there for me through the years. In the war, we had each other's back as we are sitting today. When my wife died, he preached her funeral and he kept me and my boys up in an apartment until I could move near my sister. I had to get them in another school. He never would take any money, only a handshake and a hug. I will stay till he says it is over."

They both saw the boys coming through the woods. They came up to the two men and said, "This is our turf. LEAVE!"

Lonestar stood on the table as did Haruto. "We were just leaving, sonny!"

"I ain't your sonny," and he ran at Lonestar who did not move, but grabbed his throat and the huge teenage could not move.

Haruto said loudly, "Don't kill him … these punks mean no harm … do you boys?"

Five ran at him and he took them, all five out. With one judo move after the other. They were all on the ground holding their injuries in front of Haruto.

While four ran at Lonestar, he threw the sonny boy at them. One had a gun in his jeans. He was easing it out of his pocket.

Lonestar flicked his switchblade, and stared at him before saying, "I will have this in your heart before you can fire that gun … so why don't you leave it where it is, and leave these woods the way you came in. ALIVE!"

They all scurried back to the road, and got on their bikes.

Haruto fist bumped Lonestar, and they walked back to the motel. They made a good team. Haruto introduced Lonestar to his brother Minato.

They had supper together and Haruto's wife, Machi and her sister, Mitsumi joined.

Lonestar bowed to each woman. Mitsumi was intrigued with Lonestar. Her eyes never left him. She was not engaged to Minato, so she being single was going to explore other avenues.

Mitsumi asked Lonestar, "Are you married?" She smiled sweetly.

Machi gasped because her brother-in-law was watching carefully and growling.

Lonestar said, "No, I am not," and continued eating. Then he asked, "Are you married?"

She said quietly, "No never!" and Lonestar looked at Haruto who looked at his brother.

So that was the cue to be cautious. "How about you Minato. Are you married?," He shook his head no.

Lonestar said, "Well you should be! You are about my son's age and he let a good girl slip right through his fingers. Don't let it happen to you. You'll regret it. Little lady..." He was looking at Mitsumi, "I am old enough to be your grandfather. Don't be embarrassed. Many people think I am young," he laughed which was rare.

He looked at Haruto. "I have really enjoyed the meal. Hope you will ask me again," and he went to his room.

"He is in good shape Minato. He took down five teenagers this afternoon ... and didn't even break a sweat. He is the sniper who took Shackleford out."

The women gasped, they had heard it on TV.

Minato asked, "What's he doing eating with us?"

Haruto cut his steak and ate some rice, then said, "He's a special friend of Mr. Trevor's and he is seeking ... your and my help ... to keep Bruce safe. I will talk to you later about it."

The women were talking about their needlepoint and Japanese dolls that they were working on to sell. They never wanted to think about their men being in danger, so busy work took their minds off what the men were planning.

CHAPTER THREE

Minato had been trying to get Mitsumi's attention, but she would not look his way. She walked close to her sister on the way back to her room.

Minato took her hand and turned her around, and he stared into her eyes. "The man is right you are mine. If you will have me?"

"I have loved you all my life. Are you sure, not because of a stranger's words. I do not want you unless you truly love me as Haruto loves Machi," she said.

"We need to talk more. Can you come with me?" and they went to his room. He knelt down and took the ring box from his pocket, "Will you marry me?" She almost fainted and he stood to steady her. Her lips were trembling and tears were streaming down her face.

She said, "Yes." He put the ring on her ring finger and kissed her hand.

She kissed his lips and put both arms around his neck.

"I had to work nights to get you the ring before I could ask you. You scared me tonight. I thought you were going to go after that Cherokee." He gave her the mean eye and then grabbed her and kissed her tenderly.

"He's a good man. He saw right through both of us. Now go tell your sister and stay away from me till the wedding or I will not be able to handle myself," Minato said.

"We are not waiting but one day. No longer. I do not want to get married in Japan. You have time off and we can enjoy!" she bowed to him.

"Yes dear," Minato was going to have her tomorrow night and anything her heart desires will be fine with him. MY brother said it would happen and it has. She just rubbed him with her silky skirt and it had blown his mind.

She turned around in his room looking at her ring and said, "We are in America. I will stay in here with you tonight. I will tell sister on the phone, and she will understand when she sees my ring."

He was so ready, but she did not know what she was asking.

"Calm down," he told himself.

"Machi, will understand I hope," he said.

"Don't worry I can handle her," she reassured him.

He said, "Can you handle me?" He wasn't so sure. She was so petite and so naive. He would have to plan it right.

Machi was knocking on the door and Haruto was right behind her.

Mitsumi held her ring up and it was sparkling, and it was bigger than Machi. She was examining it. "You did good Minato. My sister loves you and now I see you love her or you would not have spent your hard earn pay on this ring."

"Congrats! We are happy for you two. You both are over twenty one, so it is your choice. The parents do not have to know about tonight. The marriage license had BETTER be in your hand tomorrow, brother."

"It will ... I do love her. Your friend is a good man," Minato said and kissed his bride-to-be.

"Get out!" Minato stated they were interfering with his wedding night. His brother laughed, and her sister cried, and hugged them both.

"I need to bathe you my husband, and then you can bathe me. Our wedding night will start clean as snow." She was taking his clothes off and folding them. He was breathing very deep. This was important to her so he would endure.

He took her clothes off and she was white as porcelain and her breast were large. She had kept them strapped down, and as he took the cloth off and viewed them, his mouth fell open. They showered. If in Japan, they would have bathed in a large tub or pool. He took her in the water. She had closed her eyes. He carried her to their bed and kissed her all over her body until she wanted him close again.

"We have a life time to learn and teach each other. So tonight you tell me, if you want to sleep or explore?" he asked.

"I want my husband to be satisfied. We will explore. I have wanted you for so long and you kept saying you were not the marrying kind."

"Oh Mitsumi you are mine and you are perfect. Oh so perfect. Does it feel good?"

"I... I am about to do something. .. but I don't know why ... but I want all of you. I know you are holding back."

How did I not know what Machi and Haruto were doing in their bedroom at night? She thought to herself.

"I am about to scream and help me!"

He rode her to the top and they fell back down together.

"How much more do you need," he said.

"A lifetime!" she looked adoring into his eyes.

They cuddled together and fell asleep.

The next morning she could barely walk so he was going to do the husband thing.

He ran her a bubble bath and she soaked for an hour and he would run hot water in every fifteen minutes. When he dried her, she said, "that really helped. Thank you for taking care of me, husband."

"It's a two-way street," he kissed her.

"We need to be going to the courthouse and get the license and we can get married by the Justice of the Peace, if you want and have a big wedding when we get back to Japan?"

He stopped to kiss her again and felt those magnificent breast … one more time before she bound them. They were for his eyes only.

"Let's go get married," and out the door they went.

Corey and Jason were playing video games. Eunice was helping Madeline with fixing sandwiches and Debbie was baking chocolate chip cookies.

Tate came by sniffing deeply, "Something smells like my wife is cooking my favorite! Yes, she is … my nose never lies. I'll take this batch into the game room."

Marcus came through the door, also following his nose to Debbie.

"Tate just took a batch to the game room, but you had better run if you want any!" she said.

"My running shoes are at home. So I'll just join the pretty ladies and wait for the next batch," he winked at her.

He sat down beside Eunice and asked her how she was feeling today.

She said, "Better but this is weird ... me not being at work. I haven't missed a day in seven years this week!" She was proud of her work record. "I do appreciate you 'all taking such good care of me last night," Eunice looked at Madeline first and then at Marcus.

Madeline said, "You are so welcome. Think nothing of it!"

Marcus said, "Honey I bet you now remember my name," and they all laughed together.

She said, "How could I ever forget?"

He took her hand, "I will not let you forget ever," patting it before the boys came in.

Madeline said, "Who wants heroes?"

Jason flexed his little biceps, "I'm a hero!"

Corey punched him, "She's talking about a hero sandwich!"

"Do you want mustard or mayonnaise?" Madeline was asking everyone when Trevor walked in and said, "Mustard!"

Marcus walked over and shook his hand, "Fine Job!"

Eunice said, "Thank you so much for everything. You and Madeline have saved my family from the media frenzy. I know myself, I would have been lost. My boys said they feel like this is their second home and you are their hero."

Madeline said, "I am so glad because they have cheered Tate up. He and Debbie are really special to us!"

"Eunice can fill you in sometime, Marcus," Madeline said.

"Sounds like a dinner date to me. What do you say, honey... Will you dine with me?" he was looking at Eunice.

"I will think about it. The first one was unbelievable," she said.

They all laughed. Madeline and Trevor said at the same time, "We are not coming this time!"

"Good, I want her all to myself anyway," Marcus was gazing into Eunice's eyes. "I will have my bodyguards with us at all times, you will be safe my dear!"

"And who's going to protect her from you," Trevor was teasing.

"Now Trevor, I thought you of all people would have my back," Marcus joked.

To Be Continued

Printed in the United States
By Bookmasters